Five Nights at Freddy's™

FAZBEAR FRIGHTS #11

PRANKSTER

Five Nights at Freddy's

FAZBEAR FRIGHTS #11

PRANKSTER

BY

SCOTT CAWTHON
ELLEY COOPER
ANDREA WAGGENER

Scholastic Inc.

Photo of TV static: © Klikk/Dreamstime

All rights reserved. Published by Scholastic Inc., *Publishers since 1920.* SCHOLASTIC and associated logos are trademarks and/or registered trademarks of Scholastic Inc.

The publisher does not have any control over and does not assume any responsibility for author or third-party websites or their content.

This book is a work of fiction. Names, characters, places, and incidents are either the product of the author's imagination or are used fictitiously, and any resemblance to actual persons, living or dead, business establishments, events, or locales is entirely coincidental.

Library of Congress Cataloging-in-Publication Data available

ISBN 978-1-338-74120-9

1 2021

Printed in the U.S.A.

23

First printing 2021 • Book design by Jeff Shake

TABLE OF CONTENTS

Some nights Jeremiah felt like he was one of the last cells in a dying body. When he was hired four years ago, straight out of college, the office had been a lively, dynamic place, full of people who were full of ideas. The boss had even shown up regularly back then. The company had produced a couple of moderately successful video games, and everybody felt confident they were on the way up.

Unfortunately, they had a lousy sense of direction.

The past three years had brought an increasing number of layoffs and a decreasing amount of revenue. Jeremiah had been in the process of sending out his résumé to other potential employers when the company was suddenly bought out by Fazbear Entertainment and entrusted with the task of developing their new virtual reality game. Excited about the possibility of working with VR and hopeful that the successful franchise might bring the company new life, Jeremiah had decided to stay.

Besides, he hadn't really wanted to leave. If he left, he

Hope, in this case, referred to a person, not a quality, though Jeremiah had to admit he pinned a lot of his hopes on Hope. One of the three employees left in the office, Hope possessed every human quality Jeremiah treasured. She was kind and thoughtful without being a pushover. She was smart and resourceful without being arrogant. She was hardworking but fun-loving, too.

He didn't love Hope for her looks, but he still had to admit she was lovely to look at. Men who preferred flashier types might find her a little plain, but in Jeremiah's opinion, these guys were too obvious in their tastes to appreciate Hope's soft, natural beauty. She had shoulder-length ash-blonde hair that fell in soft waves around her keen-featured face. Her eyes were wide-set, brown, and doe-like. Her lips were delicate-looking pink petals. Jeremiah often wondered if they were as soft as they looked.

Since Jeremiah saw Hope every day, he thought that surely someday she would really see him and realize how he felt. He had tried to confess his feelings to her on two different occasions. The first time, he felt like his mouth had been superglued shut. The second time, he had gotten his mouth open, but then their only other coworker, Parker, had barged in and taken over center stage, as always. Unlike Jeremiah, Parker never had trouble finding words. Sometimes Jeremiah wished he would lose a few of them.

Jeremiah sat at his desk, working on coding the VR game, absorbed in his work. He absentmindedly lifted his thermal mug to take a sip of coffee. As soon as the liquid touched his tongue, he felt like his mouth was turning itself inside out. The taste was unbearably sour, and without even thinking, he spat it out, spraying the computer screen. "What the—"

"Oh, that was too funny!" Parker's voice boomed from the doorway. He was laughing his usual manic *hee-hee-hee*. "You did a total spit take! I got you good! Here, I got it on my phone. I'll show you."

Jeremiah looked up to see Parker, with his too-styled hair and impeccable suit, convulsed in laughter. To make it worse, Hope was standing beside him, giggling with her hand over her mouth. Her laughter, unlike Parker's, was gentle and lovely, like the pealing of a bell. Jeremiah wished that she was laughing with him over some private joke they had shared instead of laughing at him, caught in another one of Parker's stupid pranks.

Jeremiah knew he was blushing. He looked down at the mug. An acrid odor floated up from it and made his nose tingle. "What *was* that?"

Parker laughed even harder. "Apple cider vinegar! I sneaked it into your cup while you were in the restroom. Stuff's supposed to be good for you, actually, but it probably helps to know up front that it's what you're drinking."

Hope shook her head, but she was smiling. "Parker, you're terrible." Her sweet tone didn't sound negative, though. It was as though she *liked* that he was terrible.

"Check this out," Parker said. He held his phone up to Jeremiah. On the small screen, Jeremiah watched himself working obliviously, then taking in a mouthful of the vile liquid. He watched as his eyes got huge and he spat the vinegar out of his mouth, looking like an ugly stone gargoyle with a spout for a mouth. "Wow," he said, trying to sound good-natured. "You really got me there."

"You bet I did!" Parker said, running a hand through his overgelled brown forelock. He showed no signs of stopping his laughter anytime soon. "How long do you think it would take for that video to go viral?"

"Don't post it," Jeremiah said, sounding weaker and more desperate than he meant to. He was already embarrassed enough with only two people witnessing the prank.

"Here," Hope said. She took the phone out of Parker's hand and tapped the screen. "Deleted. Nobody else needs to see that but us." Her voice was soft, comforting.

Jeremiah was touched. "Thanks, Hope."

Parker nudged Hope with his elbow. "Aww, you're no fun."

"And you're very naughty." Hope dug through her purse, then walked toward Jeremiah's desk. She held a wrapped peppermint in her outstretched hand. "Here, this will get the nasty taste out of your mouth."

Jeremiah took the peppermint, letting his fingers graze the palm of Hope's hand, which was soft and smooth. Her favorite ring—an aquamarine, for her birthstone—winked in the light as she retracted her hand. He would rather take her hand than the mint, but he knew that wasn't what she was offering. "Thanks," he said again. He popped the mint into his mouth. It was sweet. Like Hope.

Parker clapped him on the back. "I got you good," he said again, chuckling. "But no hard feelings, right, buddy?"

Jeremiah looked at Parker's grinning face, his large, almost unbelievably white teeth. There was something childlike about him, mischievous but not malevolent. He couldn't stay mad at Parker. "Of course not," Jeremiah said. "But watch out. I might get *you* next."

"You think so?" Parker said with one of his *hee-hee-hee* laughs. "That's some big talk, buddy. Catch me if you can. Many have tried, but *all* have failed!" He backed out of the office as if he were reluctant to turn his back on Jeremiah.

Hope shook her head, smiling. "He's such a little boy."

"I was just thinking that exact thing," Jeremiah said. This fact made him feel strangely happy. He and Hope were so compatible, they even *thought* alike.

"I mean, he's good at his job and everything, but

emotionally . . . I'd say about eight years old." Hope sighed. There was an awkward silence that Jeremiah failed to fill, and then Hope said, "Well, I guess I'd better get back to work."

"And whose job are you doing today?" Jeremiah asked. This question was a running joke of sorts. Three years ago, Hope had been hired to work the front desk at the office, but as the number of employees decreased, she ended up doing the jobs of several other people. For no additional compensation, of course.

"Mostly the PR director's," Hope said. "Though later I think I get promoted to pretend boss for a while."

Jeremiah sat up straighter. "I'd better look out, then and try to act extra busy."

"You'd better," Hope said, flashing her lovely little smile. "You wouldn't want the pretend boss to have to pretend fire you."

Jeremiah smiled back, wishing he could think of a witty response.

"Well . . ." Hope lifted her hand in a little wave. "I'll see you, Jeremiah."

"I'm sure you will," Jeremiah said. How could Hope not see him? There were only three people on the whole floor.

But at the same time, he knew that Hope didn't *actually* see him. Not the way he wanted her to, anyway. And yet every time she was in the room, his feelings for her seemed so obvious. Whenever she approached, he felt like one of those old cartoon characters whose eyes pop out of their sockets and heart visibly beats out of their chest. But apparently she didn't see him like that. Or like much of anything at all.

Jeremiah sighed. It was time to get back to work.

Jeremiah lived in a plain, one-bedroom apartment in walking distance of the office. He had lived in much worse places when he was a student—basement apartments with ancient stained carpets and faucets that leaked more than they ran. Everything in this apartment was clean and new and in working order, but it was boring and bland and entirely devoid of character. It was a neat little box with eggshell-colored walls and beige carpet, everything designed to be as neutral and inoffensive as possible. Jeremiah knew that hanging some pictures on the wall and adding some plants or colorful cushions would help matters, but he could never gather the motivation to decorate. Something about the apartment felt temporary, like a hotel room he was staying in for a few nights, even though he had signed a one-year lease.

Tonight as soon as he got "home," if that's what this place was, he stripped off his business-casual khakis and button-down and changed into a T-shirt and a ratty but comfy pair of sweatpants. He went to the kitchen, opened the refrigerator door, and surveyed his options. He figured he should probably eat the leftover Chinese takeout before it went bad. He grabbed the white paper box, a soda, and a fork, and made his way to the couch. He reached for the remote and channel-surfed while he slurped his noodles cold out of the box.

There was an action movie that looked promising, one

he had meant to see when it was in the theater, but he hadn't gotten around to it. He polished off his noodles and watched the hero, in an expensive black suit, run and jump and beat up bad guys. He briefly pictured himself wearing the same kind of suit and punching Parker square in the face. But he knew he would never do it. He was decidedly not a man of action. He was the kind of guy who sat passively and watched the action unfold in front of him on a screen.

When the movie was over, Jeremiah changed over to a late-night talk show, but he soon dozed off. He dreamed, as he often did, about Hope. He and Hope were at a fancy restaurant with dim lighting and crisp white tablecloths. She was wearing a rose-colored dress with a scoop neck that showed off her lovely collarbones. He was wearing the same black suit as the guy in the action movie. They were eating frou-frou French desserts, pot au chocolat for her and crème brûlée for him, and they reached across the table, feeding each other sweet spoonfuls. They didn't talk because they didn't need to. Even without making a sound, they were in perfect harmony.

When the alarm on his phone went off, Jeremiah started and looked around, disoriented. He had slept in an awkward position on the couch all night. His neck hurt, and he had drooled on the upholstery. And now, like almost every other morning, it was time to make the coffee, to dutifully crunch his way through a bowl of cereal, to shower and put on clean khakis and a polo, all in preparation for another long day of work.

The dream he had enjoyed last night was definitely over.

In the shower, Jeremiah gave himself a pep talk. *Okay, so Hope is completely oblivious to your feelings, and she thinks Parker is hilarious. But you know what? You're a nice guy, and Parker, deep down, is a jerk. Didn't Mom always say that niceness counts? So maybe if you just keep on showing Hope how nice you are, she'll eventually realize she can't live without you.*

The pep talk helped a surprising amount. Jeremiah whistled as he dressed with a little more care than usual. He shaved off a three-day growth of beard and even put a little "product"—though he couldn't remember when or why he'd bought it—in his hair. He regarded himself in the mirror. Not bad. He was no action hero, but he looked nice. And he *was* nice. Nice was key.

He walked to the office with a spring in his step and took the elevator up to the fifth floor. As soon as the doors slid open, he heard the sound of Hope's laughter.

Parker was sitting at his desk showing Hope something on his computer. They were both laughing. Hope was standing right behind him looking at the screen. If either of them adjusted their positions by an inch, they would be touching.

"Hi, guys," Jeremiah said.

Neither of them turned away from whatever was on the screen.

"Hi, guys," Jeremiah said, louder this time.

"Oh, hi, Jeremiah," Hope said, favoring him with a smile. "I didn't hear you come in."

Nobody can hear much of anything if Parker's around, Jeremiah thought. But he didn't say the words. Nice. That was what he was going to be.

"Hey, Jeremiah, my man," Parker said, smiling his most disingenuous smile. "Have you had your morning cup of vinegar, or should I hook you up?"

Hope gave Parker a little play slap on the shoulder. "Now you stop that." She turned to look at Jeremiah with her big, lovely eyes. "Jeremiah, I just want you to know that I've talked to Parker, and he's promised to be on his best behavior today."

"I *did* make that promise." Parker gave a wicked grin. "The trouble is, my best behavior still isn't that good." He waggled his eyebrows theatrically.

"Well, then you're going to have to be better than your best," Hope said, though her voice still tinkled with laughter. "I mean, look at poor Jeremiah there. His nerves are shot."

At least she's looking at me, Jeremiah thought, though he wished she weren't looking at him with pity.

When Jeremiah filled his mug at the coffee station, he sniffed it to make sure it was really coffee. Even with Parker supposedly on his best behavior, you couldn't be too careful.

Jeremiah sat at his desk and started working on the game. He fell into the screen, and for a few hours, the combination of creativity and problem solving distracted him from thinking about the slim distance that separated Hope and Parker at his desk this morning.

There was a knock on his half-open door. He jumped a little even though the knock had been so light it was barely there. When he was immersed in work, returning to reality was always a little startling.

Fortunately, it was a pleasant reality to return to. Hope was standing in the doorway, smiling at him. "Sorry to break your concentration," she said. "Parker's running out for sandwiches. You want one?"

"Sure, thanks," Jeremiah said.

"Corned beef on rye with extra mustard, tortilla chips and pickle on the side?" Hope asked.

Was it pathetic how his heart leaped, hearing that she knew his sandwich order? "You know me too well," he said, smiling at her.

"It's the only kind of sandwich I've ever seen you eat," Hope said.

"Sorry I'm so predictable." Jeremiah felt suddenly sure that he was the most boring person in the world. No wonder Hope preferred the loose cannon that was Parker.

"Hey, predictable can be nice sometimes," Hope said. "In an unpredictable world, it's nice to know that a corned beef sandwich will always make you happy."

You're *what would make me happy*, Parker thought. But of course he didn't say it. He just thanked Hope for taking his lunch order, then chided himself for his weakness, for being a boring, predictable, corned-beef-on-rye-eating coward who never had the courage to speak his true feelings.

He turned to his computer and fell back into the virtual world. He was having a lot more success there than he was in the real one.

Half an hour later, Hope appeared in his doorway again. "Hey, Parker and I are going to have lunch in the break room. You want to join us?"

"Sure," Jeremiah said. He couldn't help but feel he was

being invited as an afterthought, but he couldn't say no to any gathering that included Hope.

They sat around the table in the break room. Jeremiah opened his plastic takeout box. Corned beef sandwich, tortilla chips, and a pickle. His predictable favorite.

"Hey, did anybody watch *Kingdom of Bones* last night?" Parker asked, tearing off a chunk of his roast beef sandwich with his gigantic teeth. Jeremiah was reminded of a nature documentary he saw with lions tearing off big chunks of zebra with their huge fangs. He feared that Parker was the lion here, and he was the zebra.

"It's on my DVR. I haven't watched it yet, so no spoilers," Jeremiah said.

"I don't watch that show. It's too violent for me," Hope said, delicately nibbling at a corner of her veggie wrap. She was a vegetarian because she said animals were friends, not food. Jeremiah admired her kind heart, not to mention her conviction and self-discipline. "There's already too much violence in the world. I don't like to watch it simulated for entertainment."

That was the thing about Hope, Jeremiah thought. She was a good person. She had principles.

"You're such a *girl*," Parker said in a tone that implied being a girl was a bad thing. "I bet you watch romantic comedies instead."

Hope gave a small, embarrassed-looking smile. "Sometimes, yeah."

Parker shook his head. "I would rather have my eyes burned out with a hot poker than watch a single romantic comedy."

"Well, fortunately that's probably a choice that will never come up in your life," Jeremiah said.

"Unless you date a girl who's super forceful about wanting you to watch romantic comedies," Hope said, laughing her burbling little laugh.

Jeremiah felt a little tingle of happiness. Right now it felt like he and Hope were sharing a little joke at Parker's expense. Enjoying Hope's smiling face, he absentmindedly popped a chip into his mouth.

And he was on fire. Or at least, his mouth was. It felt like someone had filled his mouth with boiling lava. His lips, his cheeks, his tongue burned with an intensity that made fat tears spring to his eyes and spill down his cheeks.

"Jeremiah, what's wrong? You've turned all red!" Hope said, getting up from the table to get closer to him.

He wanted to say "hot," but his mouth was too much of an inferno to form words. Instead he made a fanning gesture in front of his mouth, hoping it would explain his problem. He jumped up from the table, ran over to the sink, and spat out whatever it was that had turned his mouth into a volcano. He turned on the faucet, stuck his head under it, and let the cold water flow into his scalded mouth. When he lifted up his head, gasping, he turned to see Parker laughing so hard he couldn't catch his breath.

"Parker, what did you do to him?" Hope demanded. This time she wasn't sharing in Parker's laughter.

"Oh," Parker said, holding his stomach. "Oh, that was too good!"

Jeremiah filled a paper cup with water and drank it down. The fire in his mouth had died down somewhat, but it still wasn't totally extinguished. It felt like there wasn't enough water in the world to cool him all the way down.

"What happened?" Hope asked, her tone testy.

"The deli was selling hot chips," Parker said, still short of breath from laughing. "The kind people eat on a dare. I slipped one in with Jeremiah's regular tortilla chips." He doubled over in a fresh fit of giggles. "Which may have been the greatest thing I've ever done in my life!"

"Well, I doubt it was the greatest thing in Jeremiah's life," Hope said. "Those things cause people actual pain. I thought you said you were going to be on your best behavior today, Parker?"

"Well, I warned you that for me 'best behavior' means something different than it does for other people," Parker said. "You know, when I see an opportunity for fun, I take it. No regrets."

And no pity either, Jeremiah thought.

Hope stood at the refrigerator. She opened the freezer door and filled a paper cup with ice. "Well, I think you owe Jeremiah an apology."

"You know my motto: no regrets and no apologies." Parker shrugged, getting up from the table. "Once you start thinking about it, you'll realize how hilarious it was. Later, losers." He held up his finger and thumb in the shape of an *L* and strutted out of the break room.

"Here," Hope said, holding out the paper cup to Jeremiah. "Suck on some ice cubes. It'll help."

"Thanks," Jeremiah managed to say, but his voice sounded thick and strange. He felt like his lips and tongue were swelling.

"I usually think Parker's pranks are funny," Hope said. "But this one went too far. I mean, what if you had had an allergic reaction or something?"

"I'm okay," Jeremiah said, not being entirely honest.

Actually, while his mouth felt like it might never be okay again, there was something better than okay about the attention Hope was giving him. It felt like she was really noticing him, like she was taking his side over Parker's for once.

"Are you sure? I mean, are you even going to be able to work for the rest of the day?" Hope's brow was knitted with concern. On her, even worry was cute.

It was nice to know she cared.

"Oh, I'll be fine. Once I get into the game, I won't even notice I'm in the world."

"I like that about you," Hope said. "I've often thought about putting a sign on your desk that says, *Do not disturb. Genius at work.*"

So Hope thought he was a genius? Jeremiah was pretty sure he was blushing. Or maybe it was just leftover heat from the chip. "Oh, I don't know about that," he said. "You're much better with people than I am."

Hope smiled at him. "Well, then we complement each other, don't we?"

Now he *knew* he was blushing. "I guess we do."

Every Tuesday night, Jeremiah met his friends Matt and Ty to play team trivia at Leonardo's Pizza. It was Jeremiah's one regular social engagement.

Jeremiah had met Matt and Ty in college, where they

were all computer science majors who were obsessed with gaming. Back then, they would meet up in one of their dorm rooms and play for hours, fueled by soda and junk food. Most of the time, each of them was immersed in his own game on a laptop or console, though they traded enough banter back and forth that the experience was still social. When Jeremiah took a psychology class, he learned that when toddlers play in the same room but not together it was called *parallel play*. It amused him that he and his friends were in college but still engaged in parallel play.

There was no parallel play for them anymore. They were three full-grown men with grown-up jobs. Matt was married with a baby boy, and Ty had a steady girlfriend. Still, the three of them managed to meet once a week to eat pizza and play trivia and joke around in pretty much the same goofy way they had back in college.

Jeremiah walked into Leonardo's and scanned the dining room, which was decorated in what could only be called cheeseball Italian style, with framed photos of the Leaning Tower of Pisa and the Coliseum, and red-and-white-checked plastic tablecloths. Matt and Ty already had a table and waved him over. Ty's looks hadn't changed a bit since college—he was still a boyish-looking Black guy wearing the same round, gold-framed glasses he had always worn. But marriage and fatherhood had caused Matt to gain what he jokingly called his "baby weight," and there were dark circles under his eyes from exhaustion. He was genuinely starting to look like he could be somebody's dad.

"Hey, J," Ty said, gesturing for Jeremiah to sit down.

"I was just telling Ty I don't know how much help I'm going to be at team trivia tonight," Matt said, yawning theatrically. "Connor is teething, and I haven't slept for three nights."

"The joys of fatherhood, huh?" Ty said, smiling.

Matt didn't return the smile. "Just you wait, buddy."

"Oh, I *plan* to wait," Ty said. "As long as possible."

They were interrupted by the arrival of their usual server, who gave them a quick glance and rattled off, "Extra-large pepperoni and mushroom and three diet sodas?"

"And that's how you know we've been coming here too long," Ty said. After the server left, Ty turned to Jeremiah. "So how are things at your glamorous workplace?"

Both Matt and Ty had regular IT jobs with fairly boring businesses. They always playfully expressed jealousy that Jeremiah had landed a job in game development.

Jeremiah thought it was a trade-off. Sure, he had the cooler-sounding job, but unlike them, he was alone. No wife or girlfriend, no kids, not even a pet.

"It's not that glamorous," Jeremiah said. "It feels like we're just barely keeping afloat in a tiny life raft. I hope this VR game is a big seller. It would be good for things to be on the upswing again." He thought of his day at work, the hidden hot chip, followed by Hope's protectiveness of him and her saying that the two of them complemented each other. "But I think things may be looking up with Hope."

He relayed the whole story of his and Hope's interactions and followed it with "So what do you think?"

"It sounds . . . Hope-ful," Matt said, then laughed for far too long at his terrible pun.

Ty rolled his eyes. "Ignore Matt and his horrible dad jokes. I think it sounds like she definitely cares about you, man. She may not be totally into you yet, but the thing she said about you complementing each other sounds promising."

"Why say *promising* when you can say *Hope-ful*?" Matt said.

"I think you're so tired you're punchy," Ty said to Matt.

"Don't you mean *pun*-chy?" Matt was cracking himself up.

"As your sane friend—unlike this one," Ty said, chucking Matt on the shoulder, "I say you should ask her out."

"Yeah, but what if she says no?" Jeremiah's stomach knotted in anxiety.

"Well, that would suck, but at least you would've had the courage to ask her," Ty said. "Nothing ventured, nothing gained."

"But what would the courage be worth? Especially if I have to see her at work every day after she turns me down?" Jeremiah couldn't imagine the awkwardness. And then, too, if Parker got wind of the fact that Hope had rejected Jeremiah, he would never let Jeremiah forget it.

"I can tell by the look on your face that you're

worrying about problems you don't have yet," Ty said. "Just ask her out."

Matt began rhythmically pounding on the table and chanting. "Ask. Her. Out. Ask. Her. Out."

Ty joined him, and Jeremiah, laughing, finally said he'd think about it. But his friends only stopped pounding on their table when the pizza arrived.

Looking in the bathroom mirror, Jeremiah ran the razor over his foamy face. "Today's the day," he told his reflection. "I'm going to do it. I'm going to ask her out."

He splashed warm water on his chin, dried off, and combed his hair. He looked himself over, something he hardly ever did. *Not bad*, he decided. True, he wasn't slick or handsome like Parker, but there was also something about Parker's face that made it seem exceptionally punchable. Jeremiah at least looked like a nice guy.

He *was* a nice guy, he told himself. He would be an excellent boyfriend if given the chance.

He put on an extra coat of deodorant because he knew the anxiety would make him sweaty. He squirted toothpaste on his toothbrush, and as he brushed, he remembered Matt and Ty's rhythmic chant as they pounded on the table at Leonardo's: *Ask. Her. Out. Ask. Her. Out.*

As he walked down the sidewalk to work, his feet pounded out the rhythm of their chant: *Ask. Her. Out. Ask. Her. Out.*

You need to ask her as soon as possible, he lectured himself. *Don't sit around all day trying to talk yourself into it. Just jump right in and ask.*

He took out his phone and texted Matt and Ty. **I'm gonna ask her.**

Matt replied with a **Go for it!**

Ty sent a thumbs-up.

Jeremiah smiled. He was ready.

On the elevator, he kept his fingers crossed that when he entered the office he would find Hope alone so they could talk. But when the doors slid open, he saw that he had no such luck.

"Oh, good, he's here!" Parker said. He was standing with Hope, who was looking heartbreakingly pretty in a robin's egg–blue blouse that somehow made her eyes look even bigger and browner. Both Parker and Hope were holding VR headsets.

"Hi, guys," Jeremiah muttered, trying to hide his disappointment.

"Hey, dude," Parker said. "We were wondering if you could open up the testing room and get things running. I want to do a practice run on the game so far, and I thought Hope could help me."

It was the exact opposite of the situation Jeremiah had wished for. Basically, Parker was asking Jeremiah for the privilege of being sealed in a dark room alone with Hope. "You want me to help out, too?" Jeremiah asked, fearing he already knew the answer.

"No, it'd be better if you stayed out here and monitored things on the computer," Parker said, grinning his loathsome grin. "I figure Hope will bring a fresh take on things since she's not actually working on the game development. She can experience it cold, from a player's perspective."

"Right," Jeremiah said. "Well, let me get things set up." He used his key card to open the door to the practice room and then sat down in front of his computer. How could he have been feeling so good when he woke up this morning and yet feel so despondent now?

"Okay, Hopey, ready to have some fun?" Parker asked, sounding like a demented game show host.

Also, where did he get off calling her *Hopey*? It sounded like *dopey*. He hated it.

"Sure," Hope said, giggling.

They disappeared into the testing room, and Parker shut the door behind them.

Jeremiah tried to concentrate on his work, but for once, he couldn't. He felt sick. Every couple of minutes, he heard a stray chuckle coming from the testing room. The intimate-sounding laughter made his mind go places he didn't want it to go. *Stop it*, he ordered himself. *They're playing the game, that's all. Of course they're laughing. People tend to laugh after a good jump scare.*

But then the what-ifs . . . started. *What if they're not playing the game? What if they're laughing because they're flirting with each other? What if it's more than flirting? What if his greasy mouth is pressed up against her petal-like lips? What if his slimy paw is stroking her wavy, lustrous hair?* The more Jeremiah didn't want to picture these things, the more he saw them.

By the time Parker and Hope emerged laughing and disheveled from the testing room, Jeremiah was a shaky, sweaty mess. "You know what?" he said. "I may go on home. I think I've picked up a little bug or something."

"You look a little gray," Hope said, sounding concerned.

"I feel it," Jeremiah said.

"Wow, you must," Parker added. "You never miss work."

"I know." Jeremiah was already on his feet and putting on his jacket. "But I just can't . . . be here."

"Well, rest up so you can be sure to come in tomorrow!" Parker said.

The last thing he saw before closing the door was Hope, biting her lower lip like she did when she was excited about something.

At home, Jeremiah put on his pajamas and got into bed just as he would if he were really sick. But he was really sick, wasn't he? He was heartsick, and that had to count. He would happily take a stomach bug or a bad cold over how he felt now.

Lying in bed, Jeremiah couldn't imagine a time in his life when he wouldn't be alone. And then he remembered something that under the present circumstances made him even more miserable: Tomorrow was his birthday.

As Jeremiah plowed through his cereal without really tasting it, he decided the easiest thing to do would be to pretend it *wasn't* his birthday. Certainly nobody at the office would remember. Parker and Hope would probably be too busy canoodling in the dark testing room to even know he was there. If he just pretended this was another ordinary day at work, maybe he could avoid the nagging disappointment of a forgotten birthday. If he ignored it first, he couldn't be that upset that other people were ignoring it, too, right?

Jeremiah's phone vibrated. He picked it up to see a text from his mom: **Happy birthday! Wish I could be there for Pancakes and Presents. Gift card in the mail.** As he was replying with a thanks and a heart emoji, memories of his childhood birthdays flooded back to him.

Jeremiah had always been so excited to see what his birthday presents were that he couldn't wait without feeling like he was going to explode. Finally, probably to save herself from spending a nerve-racking day with an overexcited child, his mom had started the tradition of Pancakes and Presents. Since Jeremiah always woke up early on his birthday (Who could sleep with all that excitement?), his mom started the tradition of making him a big birthday breakfast: the cheesy scrambled eggs he liked, bacon, and a stack of buttermilk pancakes with a candle in them. After he ate breakfast, he could open his presents.

It had been a stroke of genius on his mom's part, really. That way, he had had all day to play with his new toys or games instead of spending the day pestering her about when he could tear into his gifts. On the evening of his birthday, Mom and Dad had always taken him and a friend of his choosing to Freddy's for pizza and games.

Jeremiah felt himself tearing up a little at the thought of those perfect birthdays of his past. There were no birthdays like childhood birthdays. After all that fun and fanfare, adult birthdays always felt disappointing.

Maybe he should have gone out for pancakes this morning.

He hadn't noticed it was raining until he stepped outside his apartment building. He cast a glance back inside. His umbrella was in his apartment, six floors up. It didn't seem worth the trouble to go back up and get it. He zipped up his jacket and walked in that strange, hunched way people walk when it's raining on them.

On the elevator, he tried to mentally prepare himself for the scene he was going to walk into today. Would Hope and Parker be tittering over something at Parker's desk? Would they already be locked in the testing room? Would they announce their engagement?

Don't get caught up in the drama, he told himself. *Just do your job and go home. Maybe you can order takeout and watch a movie or something.*

When the elevator doors slid open, Jeremiah was genuinely surprised by what he saw. The office was lit by strings of tiny fairy lights. A huge banner with balloons surrounding it said, HAPPY BIRTHDAY, JEREMIAH!

He smiled. They had remembered. Or even better, *she* had remembered.

But there was nobody around. Were they waiting to jump out and yell "Surprise"? Had they not heard him come in?

"Hey, guys," Jeremiah said, loud enough for his voice to carry to wherever they were hiding. "Thanks. This is really nice."

There was no answer, no movement, no sign of anyone being there but him.

He walked down the hall to the break area. On the table where the now-infamous Hot Chip Lunch had taken place, a birthday cake sat, looking just like he remembered from childhood: a white-frosted grocery store bakery sheet cake trimmed with piped royal blue icing. HAPPY BIRTHDAY, JEREMY was written in blue icing on top. He smiled. It was close enough. And whoever had put the candles on—Hope, probably—had put on the right number.

Maybe he had been wrong about adult birthdays. If someone, especially someone you loved, demonstrated thoughtfulness, then birthdays could be magical at any age.

But where was everybody? He walked the rest of the way down the hall, peeking inside empty offices and conference rooms.

Maybe they were waiting to jump out when he least expected it. He had to hand it to them. They were doing an awfully good job at hiding.

"Hope? Parker?" he called. "You can come out. You've already surprised me enough!"

There was no response.

Not knowing what else to do, Jeremiah went to his desk. Maybe they were waiting for him to get deeply immersed in his work, then they were going to jump out and surprise him.

"Jeremiah." The voice was coming from the loudspeaker, which was never used since their office staff had dwindled to such a small number. The voice sounded deep and electronic, like when people are interviewed anonymously on TV and don't want anybody to hear their real voice.

But there was no doubt in Jeremiah's mind who the distorted voice belonged to. He knew that Parker had decided to make him the victim of a birthday prank.

He hoped it was a good-natured prank at least.

"Jeremiah," the distorted voice repeated, "I have taken your coworkers Parker and Hope hostage. If you call the police, I will kill them immediately."

"Uh-huh," Jeremiah said, sounding as unconvinced as he felt. The distorted voice was obviously Parker's.

"You have a choice to make, Birthday Boy. You can flee the building with the confidence that you will live to see another birthday even though your friends won't. Or you can try to save your friends. If you take this option, you have thirty minutes. The longer you take, the worse shape they'll be in when you find them. Now, what is your choice?"

"I choose to save my friends," Jeremiah said with a sigh. In truth, he considered Parker a bully, not a friend. But he wanted to make a good impression on Hope, and triumphing over one of Parker's pranks seemed like a good way to do it. Plus, it was just a stupid game anyway, right? Like those escape rooms people chose to get themselves locked into so they could have the fun of finding the clues that would get them out.

It was his birthday after all. He might as well play a game.

"Very well," the distorted voice said. "Use your time wisely, or your friends may be missing a few pieces. Your time starts . . . NOW."

Jeremiah stood up. He had to hand it to Parker. This was certainly darker and more imaginative than his usual pranks. He looked around the workroom, trying to find clues. He looked on top of Parker's desk and even pulled the drawers open and looked inside. Nothing out of the ordinary. He went to the reception desk where Hope usually kept her stuff. Her purse was stored in the usual drawer, which meant she had definitely come in this morning. He wouldn't stoop so low as to invade her privacy by digging through her purse.

So Hope was somewhere in the building because her purse was here. And he knew Parker was here because he had heard him on the loudspeaker. To win this game—to beat Parker and impress Hope—he had to turn himself into a combination of an action hero and a sharp-minded detective. What was it Sherlock Holmes used to say in the stories Jeremiah had liked back in his middle school days? *The game is afoot.*

"Since you're at a desk, you might as well write something down," the distorted voice over the loudspeaker boomed. "Your first clue is an anagram. Write it down: STINGER MOOT."

"Stinger moot?" Jeremiah yelled back at the voice on the loudspeaker. Parker's voice. "That doesn't make any sense."

"It doesn't have to make sense," the voice bellowed. "It's an anagram. You're wasting precious time, Jeremiah.

Write it down. S-T-I-N-G-E-R space M-O-O-T."

Jeremiah did as he was told, but he wasn't going to let Parker intimidate or pressure him. Not this time. He wanted Hope to see the kind of person he really was, that he wasn't just a hapless foil for Parker's pranks.

Anagrams. It had been a long time since Jeremiah had thought about anagrams. Those were the ones where the letters were scrambled up, weren't they? He looked at the nonsensical combination of words. If this was truly a clue, then it was probably directing him to a location in the building. He spotted the letters R-O-O-M quickly, so *room* must be the second word. With those letters eliminated, it didn't take him long to figure out that the remaining letters could be rearranged to spell *testing*.

"The testing room," he said, feeling an undeniable sense of accomplishment. "I need to go to the testing room."

He walked instead of running. He didn't want Parker to think he was feeling pressured. It was just a game, after all.

He used his key card to open the door to the testing room, then turned on the light.

In the middle of the floor sat a small gift box, the size that most often contained jewelry. The little box was wrapped in colorful paper with a shiny purple bow on top. So this was a birthday treasure hunt with a horror/suspense theme? Jeremiah could live with that. At least he could say that this birthday wasn't like every other day.

He walked across the room, crouched down, and picked up the small box. He unwrapped it carefully just in case there might be a clue written on the inside of the wrapping paper. The hinged box was a deep crimson, flocked with velvet, the kind of box that might cradle an engagement ring. He flipped the lid open.

His stomach lurched.

Teeth. The velvet-lined box was filled with teeth. Some large, some perhaps small enough to be baby teeth. One molar was flecked with blood on the bottom where it had been yanked out by the root. Jeremiah wanted to keep his cool but couldn't help but visibly shudder.

Where had Parker managed to get teeth, of all things? Was he friends with a dentist who had a sick sense of humor?

Jeremiah took a deep breath. *A clue*, he told himself. *The teeth are supposed to be a clue. Stop freaking out and start thinking.*

He didn't want to touch the teeth, but he knew he needed to examine them for possible clues. He took a tissue from his pocket, spread it over the palm of his left hand, and shook the teeth onto the tissue. They contained no distinguishing markings or features. There were seven of them. Could the number be significant? Seven certainly didn't feel like a lucky number when it referred to a bunch of extracted teeth.

He set the teeth aside and examined the box. He pulled out the velvet liner. In the bottom of the box was a small piece of paper that had been folded into a tiny square. Jeremiah unfolded the paper. On it, a typed message read:

SINK YOUR TEETH INTO THIS CLUE, JEREMIAH!
GIVE ME ONE, AND I'LL MAKE MORE.
EACH ONE LIKE THE ONE BEFORE.
WHAT AM I?

Jeremiah didn't have to think for long. He had always been good at riddles. "That's easy. The copying machine."

"Don't get too confident, Jeremiah," the distorted voice boomed out of the loudspeaker, making him jump. "The time is ticking away. Only twenty minutes left. And the slower you are, the more they'll suffer. I wonder . . . if you do manage to find your friends, will you even be able to recognize them?"

"You're really enjoying this, aren't you, Parker?" Jeremiah said as he exited the testing room, leaving the teeth behind. "Stop nagging me. I'm on my way to the copy room."

In no particular hurry, Jeremiah made his way down the dark hallway.

The copy room was the third door on the left. When he walked inside, lights from the machine emanated an eerie glow. At first he went to the machine itself, but found nothing out of the ordinary. He scanned the room. It was small, so there weren't many hiding places. Other than the machine, there was just a wastebasket, a recycling bin, and a long table where people could collate their copies. He looked on the table and saw only the usual office supplies: a cup holding pens and scissors, a stapler, a small jar of paper clips.

Wait. Those aren't paper clips.

They were small, translucent ovals, white-tipped on the top and flecked with red on the bottom.

Fingernails. They're fingernails. And not fingernail clippings but whole fingernails that had been . . . removed, somehow.

Jeremiah felt the bile rising in his throat. He gagged.

He took a deep breath and told himself to calm down. These couldn't be real fingernails. They were props—extremely realistic props, the kind you'd see in a horror movie with a decent budget, but props nonetheless. He supposed it wasn't so outrageous that Parker could get his hands on such things. You could buy anything off the internet these days.

But where was the next clue? There was nothing else unusual on the table. With a shaky hand, he picked up the jar of "fingernails." He upended it, scattering the nails across the table. A small, folded piece of paper fell out of the bottom of the jar. He didn't like touching it since it had been in the jar with all those fingernails, but he knew it was the next clue, and he wasn't going to chicken out now. He wouldn't give Parker the satisfaction. He unfolded the slip of paper and read: YOU NAILED THIS CHALLENGE! Jeremiah could almost hear Parker's annoying *hee-hee-hee*. He kept reading: YOUR NEXT CLUE CONTAINS EVEN MORE FRIGHTS/TO GET THERE YOU JUST NEED TO FOLLOW THE LIGHTS.

Jeremiah stepped out into the hall. A string of tiny lights was stretched from the doorway of the copy room down the hall. He followed them, which was certainly easier than deciphering another cryptic clue. Maybe he was getting close to the end of the game. It hadn't been fun—it was too disturbing for that—but it had been interesting. He would definitely come out of this experience with a story to tell.

"Time's a-wasting, Jeremiah," the voice on the loudspeaker announced. "Only ten minutes left. Better get to your friends soon, or they'll be all to pieces!" The laughter sounded like a distorted version of Parker's *hee-hee-hee*.

"You really put some work into this, Parker, I'll give you that," Jeremiah said.

The lights stopped at a doorway to a conference room that hadn't been used since the company's downsizing. He turned the knob and walked in.

Sitting on the table, lined up as if staring at him, were three eyeballs. Two of them, Jeremiah noticed, had brown irises; the third one was blue. Seeing intact eyeballs separated from their owners made Jeremiah think of how delicate the eye was, soft and squishable, like a peeled grape. He felt a wave of nausea, a sensation that was now becoming familiar.

These eyes had to be real. Even an excellent special effects artist couldn't make something this convincing. So where was Parker getting this stuff?

A thought popped into Jeremiah's head that explained everything. On the third floor of their building there was a medical supply company. Jeremiah had never thought that much about what kind of supplies they provided—he had thought scrubs and maybe masks and gloves, that kind of thing. But what if they dealt with medical waste? Body parts left over from surgeries that were going to be sent to medical schools for study and dissection? If so, Parker could have just bought some spare parts from them.

Jeremiah felt better suddenly, confident that no one had been harmed in the creation of this elaborate prank. He spotted a slip of paper sticking out from under the blue eyeball. He didn't want to touch it, so he nudged it with the blunt end of a ballpoint pen. The eye rolled back, and he grabbed the note and unfolded it: I SEE THAT YOU'RE MOVING CLOSER TO YOUR GOAL. FOLLOW THE LIGHTS TO MAKE THINGS RIGHT!

A new string of lights started at the conference room doorway and led farther down the hall. They stopped at the office, which had belonged to the PR person before she was laid off. He tried the door and walked inside.

A medium-sized gift sat on the desk. It was wrapped in white paper decorated with shiny multicolored letters spelling HAPPY BIRTHDAY and topped with a big silver bow.

Jeremiah was starting to lose the pleasure he had always felt in unwrapping gifts.

Still, he tore through the paper and lifted the lid off the box.

Resting inside a nest of light blue tissue paper was a pile of fingers—maybe as many as twelve or thirteen, but it was hard to say because many of them had been chopped into fragments. Two of them were missing fingernails.

Jeremiah couldn't help it. Prank or no prank, he vomited into the wastebasket.

Once he was able to normalize his breathing, he

looked inside the box again. One of the fingers was small and obviously had belonged to a female. It was wearing a delicate silver ring with a light blue gemstone in it.

Aquamarine. Hope's birthstone.

He realized with horror that it was Hope's ring, the one she always wore on her right ring finger. Did this mean that the severed finger belonged to Hope? He bent over to examine it more closely. There was a small, dark freckle just below the finger's first joint.

Jeremiah had spent so much time looking at Hope that he had memorized her face, her hair, her hands. This was not her freckle, not her finger. He felt a brief moment of relief, but then felt bad for feeling relieved. Even if none of these fingers were Hope's, they were still human fingers. This had gone beyond a prank. It was a sick game, and it had gone too far. Jeremiah had often said that Parker didn't know when to stop. He was only realizing now how true that statement was.

And even if it wasn't Hope's finger, it was still Hope's ring. What did that mean? Could Hope be in some kind of danger? Was Parker hurting her?

"Enough is enough, Parker!" Jeremiah yelled. The game had gone on too long. "This needs to stop now!"

"Feeling like things are getting out of *hand*?" the voice on the loudspeaker said, laughing. "There's only one way that this game ends. Follow the lights before it's too late for your friends."

Jeremiah ran. Before, he didn't want to let Parker see him sweat, but if Hope was truly in danger, he had to get to her. He had wasted too much time already.

The lights ended at another empty office, the large one occupied by the boss when he actually bothered to show up. Jeremiah couldn't even remember when the last time had been. On the large oak desk was a cardboard box with two round holes cut into the lid. A note attached to the box said, *For the key to where your friends hide, roll up your sleeves and reach inside.*

Jeremiah pushed up his shirtsleeves and plunged his hands through the two holes in the box. Instantly, he was up to his wrists in something cold, wet, and squishy.

It would be more accurate to say some *things* that were cold, wet, and squishy because the more Jeremiah felt around in the depths of the box, the more he became aware that he wasn't just feeling one slimy mass, but individual items. His hands were tangled up long, snaky tubes. *Intestines.*

Jeremiah hoped that the innards he was feeling had come from some unfortunate livestock and had been acquired at a butcher's shop. But in his mind, he knew better.

The medical supply company, he told himself. *All this stuff came from the medical supply company. It was from people who had died from natural causes, who donated their bodies to scientific research.*

But even as he tried to convince himself, the words were sounding more and more desperate and ridiculous. If these body parts were for study or dissection, wouldn't they be preserved in some way? All the parts he had encountered during this horrible game seemed disturbingly . . . *fresh.*

Jeremiah feared he might be losing his mind. Was this how you lost the game, by losing your sanity?

He fought off wave after wave of nausea to rummage through the offal in search of the key. Finally, his right hand felt something hard and metallic. He grabbed it and withdrew his arms from the holes in the box. When he looked at his hands, they were stained red past the wrists.

He held up the key. "Okay, I've got the key! Is the game over? Do I win now? Because I am done! Do you hear me, Parker? I'm done!"

"What quest ends with just finding a key, Jeremiah?" the voice on the loudspeaker boomed. "Don't you have to find out what it's a key to? Don't you want to save your friends . . . or what's left of them?"

"You're not my friend, Parker!" Jeremiah yelled. It felt like something he should have said a long time ago.

But Hope was his friend. And she could be in danger or in pain. If she needed saving, he could do it.

He took the key and closed the office door behind him, staining the doorknob with a bloody handprint.

The trail of lights continued. He followed.

The next room had probably been an office at some point, but now it was crammed full of old office furniture. Sitting on an obviously broken desk chair was another box, wrapped for his birthday, this time with a candy-pink bow. It was a medium-sized, flat box, the kind that he had always opened last at Christmas as a kid because he had known it contained clothing, not toys or games.

He was pretty sure this box did not contain clothing.

He didn't want to open it, didn't want to see what was inside, but if he was going to play the game all the way through on the chance of saving Hope, he had no choice.

He tore off the brightly colored wrapping paper and lifted off the box's cardboard lid.

When he saw what was inside, he screamed. He tried to muffle the scream with his fist but tasted the blood that still covered his hands. He looked at the contents of the box, driven by a need to make sense of what he had seen.

Jeremiah was looking at a face that had been stripped from a human skull along with part of the scalp and hair. It took him a moment longer to recognize who the face belonged to. But then he started to put the pieces together—the brown hair with the distinctive forelock, the full lips that had so often been stretched into a self-satisfied smile. He almost expected the lips to part in a *hee-hee-hee*.

"You still think this is Parker?" the distorted voice on the loudspeaker said.

"No," Jeremiah said, surprised to hear the sob in his voice. "No. Parker's right here." He didn't want to, but he found himself looking again at Parker's peeled-away face. Jeremiah wiped tears from his eyes.

If Parker wasn't running this sick show, then who was? Jeremiah realized that as long has he had thought Parker was in charge, he could entertain the notion that no matter how bad or cruel things seemed, it was all an elaborate prank. But now it became clear that this was no prank.

It was real.

There was only one word that made sense to Jeremiah right now: *Run.*

He ran, ignoring the trail of lights, ignoring everything except what appeared to be the quickest route out of the building. The halls took on a mazelike quality. To the left, to the right, with no seeming way of escape. He reached the elevator and pushed the button. No light came on. Clearly whatever psychopath he was dealing with had tampered with the elevator. He ran for the stairwell.

He opened the door marked STAIRS. Jeremiah had always found the dimly lit stairwell creepy, even under much calmer circumstances, but there was no time to reflect on his feelings now. There was only time to run.

As he made his way down the first flight of stairs, he noticed a red smear across the white cinder-block wall. Blood. Relatively fresh blood, judging from its brightness. But whose blood was it? He couldn't slow down to think about it, or the blood that next spattered the walls could be his.

Down, down, down, he ran. Down fifteen flights of stairs, sweating, panting, his heart pounding like a snare drum. He checked the doors on the way down in hopes of being able to access the elevator from another floor. Locked. Locked. Locked. Finally, he reached the door marked *1*, the door that led to the lobby and the exit. He pushed it.

It didn't budge.

He pushed again.

It appeared to have been locked from the other side. He

pounded on the door with both fists. "Help!" he yelled. "Help me! I'm trapped in here!" He hoped he could at least get a security guard's attention.

But there was no one there to hear him.

He pounded and yelled a few more minutes just in case, but it was no use. He wiped tears of frustration from his eyes. *Now what?*

There was no place to go but back up.

Jeremiah was beyond winded. Going up the stairs was much more tiring than going down. He stopped on the landing of the sixth floor to catch his breath and saw something he hadn't noticed on the way down.

The sixth-floor door was outlined in a string of tiny lights, the same kind that had lit his way throughout the horrendous birthday game.

He pushed on the door. It opened.

Jeremiah went inside the sixth floor, an office space that had been vacant since he had taken the job with the game company. He knew going inside was probably a bad idea—no, was *definitely* a bad idea—but what other choice did he have? He could go back up to his office, which was littered with viscera and ruled by a malevolent presence on the loudspeaker, or he could take his chances here.

The only illumination on the sixth floor came from the strings of tiny lights hung along the ceiling. There were no computers, no office furniture, no other signs of human activity. There were only the tiny lights leading down a dark hallway. At the end of the hallway was some kind of faint glow.

Almost as if he had been hypnotized to do so, Jeremiah followed the lights. He was going to see this thing through.

The glow was coming from a room at the end of the hall. As he drew nearer, the source of the glow became obvious. An old TV, the kind he could remember from his grandmother's house, was sitting in the empty room. It was turned on, but the screen showed only the black-and-white pattern his grandmother had always referred to as "snow." On the shelf below the TV was an equally ancient piece of audiovisual equipment, a VCR. Jeremiah hadn't seen one of those since his childhood.

The green power button on the VCR glowed in a reassuringly familiar way. On a whim, Jeremiah pressed PLAY.

The "snow" on the screen disappeared and was replaced by the smiling faces of Parker and Hope. "Surprise!" Hope said, laughing in her soft, tinkly way.

"Got ya!" Parker said. "Got you good this time. Oh and—" He looked over at Hope.

"HAPPY BIRTHDAY!" the two of them yelled together.

"I hope you appreciate all our efforts, Jeremiah," Hope said. "It was a lot of work putting all this together, even though it was totally worth it."

"I never thought we'd get it put together in time," Parker said. "Between setting up the motion sensors and the loudspeaker—"

"But it couldn't have gone better, could it?" Hope said, flashing her familiar, sweet-looking smile.

Jeremiah didn't recognize the room in which Hope and Parker had been filmed. It was too dark to make out much of the setting; however, he could discern what was on the table at which they stood: the kind of sharp kitchen scissors used for boning meat, a variety of knives ranging in size from a small scalpel to a huge cleaver.

"It was perfect," Parker said to Hope; then he turned to face the camera. "But now that you've had your birthday surprise, there's a good chance that Hope and I need to get to a hospital!" He grinned like a game show host.

"I bet we do," Hope said, laughing.

The smile faded from Parker's face. "Okay, Parker!" he yelled into the camera. "He's ready! Give us a knock!"

Knock. Knock.

At first Jeremiah thought the knocking was coming from the videotape, but then he realized the source of the noise was a supply closet a few feet away from him. Someone—*something?*—was knocking very low on the closet door from the inside. Without even thinking about it, Jeremiah started backing out of the room, though his gaze was still fixed on the TV screen.

"Now if you'll excuse us," the Parker on the video said, "Hope and I have some work to do!" Parker leaned over toward the camera. He was holding a big pair of pliers, which he opened and closed menacingly, then let out his trademark *hee-hee-hee.*

The screen went black.

Jeremiah stood, frozen in confusion and terror, as the supply closet door slowly inched open.

"**Y**ou're not going to be a kid forever, Joel!"

"As if I'd want to be," Joel muttered.

He was just a few steps from his pickup. Two more seconds. That was all he'd needed to get to his ride and get away before he was caught. Two freaking seconds.

Joel sighed with enough volume, head roll, and shoulder action to communicate his annoyance, and he turned to glare at his dad. "What now?"

"It's only 5:53."

He decided to play dumb. "Your point?"

"You're off at 6:00, not 5:53?"

"You're nagging me about seven minutes?"

Joel's dad looked up at the hazy blue sky for a minute and then wiped the back of his hand across his forehead. His palm, of course, was perfectly clean. How'd he do that?

Joel had been working at "the family business"—as his mother liked to call his *dad's* business—D'Agostino's Nursery and Garden Center, after school and every summer since he'd turned fourteen. The job had been four years of near-daily torture—shoveling, lifting, carting, weeding, and saying "Yes, ma'am" and "Yes, sir" and "Whatever you'd like" when what he really wanted to say was . . . well, something totally different and not even a little polite.

Ever since he had started working for his dad, Joel had smelled like sweat and dirt or, worse, manure. His mother, who used to tell him daily how much she loved him, had replaced her "I love you" with "Take a shower, Joel." When he'd complain that it wasn't his fault that he smelled all the time (it was the stupid job), she countered with "Your dad's been running D'Agostino's for twenty-five years, and he never goes around stinking like a cow turd steaming in a mud puddle."

Yeah, his dad. The perfect man. The one everyone loved. The guy who never sweat. The dude who was so *special* that dirt and fertilizer didn't have the audacity to touch him.

Joel blinked and realized his dad was talking. He tuned in to the words and came in mid-sentence:

". . . think you're going to find an employer who isn't going to care you leave work a few minutes early every day? You can't be irresponsible forever. God knows I've cut you more slack than I should have. Your mother kept asking me to go easy on you. And what's that gotten us? An eighteen-year-old who acts like an eight-year-old, that's what. You're a screw-up, Joel, a total screw-up."

Joel took a deep breath and wrinkled his nose at the sickly sweet smell of cherry blossoms, which were blooming late this year for some reason. They kept dripping pink bits all over the nursery, which the breeze would then pick up and blow around. Joel's dad insisted on a "clean" nursery, which meant no fallen blossoms were allowed to litter the property. Joel had probably swept up several million of the damn things today alone.

Joel put his hands on his narrow hips—several girls had told him he looked "gorgeous" when he did that. He cocked his head at his dad. "Are you done yet?"

His dad threw up his hands and bellowed, "You're fired!"

Joel frowned. Okay, so he hated the job. However, his dad paid him two dollars an hour above any other wage Joel had been able to find, and at least the job was a day-time job. Everything else he'd looked into required working late nights, which would cut into his time with the band. Until he could skip town, which wasn't going to be until graduation, two long months away, the truth was that working at the nursery was the best job he had available at the moment. And he had to have a job. He couldn't pile up the money he needed to get to LA if he didn't keep working.

He faced his dad. "You can't fire me because I'm leaving work seven minutes early."

Steve D'Agostino looked around as feigned confusion crossed his dark face. Joel blinked; he'd just gotten that weird feeling he sometimes felt when he looked at his dad, like he was looking at an older version of himself. When his dad widened his brown eyes like that, he looked a lot like Joel, who'd received most of his strong features from his dad but whose eyes were as big and heavily lashed as his mom's. It was a good combination. Once, a lady had come up to him in the grocery store to ask if he was a model. That, in fact, was something he planned to do when he got to LA. It would support him while he got his music career going.

"Am I suffering under a delusion here?" Joel's dad asked. "Is it not true that as the *owner* of this place, I can do whatever I darn well please? Is there some other boss around here I haven't heard about? Some *dude*"—he was mimicking Joel's frequent use of the word—"who gets to call the shots?"

"Funny, *dude*," Joel said. "I'm just saying it's stupid to fire someone for leaving seven minutes early."

"You think so, huh?" His dad's voice was louder now. "Let's do the math, shall we?"

Joel looked around to see if anyone was watching him get lectured like a dumb little kid. A couple old biddies were inspecting the leaves on the cherry trees at the edge of the parking lot. A family was clustered around the plastic pinwheel lawn ornaments near the front door of the garden center. At the far side of the nursery, Joel's coworker, Seth, shoveled beauty bark into the back of one of the delivery trucks. Good. No one of consequence was around.

Joel glanced at his watch. It was now 6:00 p.m. He interrupted his dad's droning calculations and tapped his watch. "Well, now I'm not leaving early."

"You think you're a funny guy, don't you?" Joel's dad shook his head. "I don't *need* to do the math. I've already done it. Over the time you've spent working for me, I've paid you more than sixty-seven hours beyond what you've actually worked. That's easily a thousand dollars you got for doing absolutely nothing."

Joel shrugged. "So what? I'm your son. You owe me."

Joel's dad stared at Joel for ten solid seconds. After the first three, Joel thought about getting in his truck and leaving. But for some reason, he couldn't look away from his dad.

When Joel was little, he'd thought his dad was the coolest guy on the planet. Unlike his friends' dads, Joel's dad was big and broad-shouldered and fit, kind of like a superhero. He didn't drive a boring old sedan like other dads; he drove a great big shiny black truck. His dad also didn't wear typical fatherly attire, like drab khakis and polo shirts either. When Joel's dad wasn't at the nursery, he dressed in flashy clothes—dressy slacks and bright shirts and patterned ties. People around town loved Steve D'Agostino: he could make a crowd erupt in laughter, charm any woman, befriend anyone he wished. At home, he was funny and attentive; when Joel was a kid, his dad had been *fun*. Father and son would spend the summers joking around and doing cool things together. Joel's dad played guitar, and he taught his son early on, instilling in him a love of music. He even bought Joel a drum set when Joel asked for one, and they'd formed a two-person "rock band."

Something weird had happened, though, when Joel had reached his teens. The rules changed. He was no longer allowed to play and do whatever he wanted to do. His dad expected something of Joel that he just couldn't give. His dad wanted him to stop having fun. He wanted Joel to "get serious" and "grow up."

After a while, Joel stopped fighting it. By sophomore year, he was *all for* growing up because it meant he could get away from his smothering parents and this backward small town. It meant he could go play music where someone would appreciate him instead of yelling at him for it. But why did growing up have to mean getting serious? Why did he have to stop having fun?

Joel blinked when he felt a tug and heard a rip. He looked down. "What the—"

His dad had just torn the name tag off Joel's shirt with such force, it left a hole.

"I'm done with you," his dad said. "Just get out of here."

Joel felt blood flood his face. His temples throbbed. He clenched his fists.

"Now," his dad growled.

Joel threw up his hands. "Fine." He turned and yanked open the door of his pickup.

Joel flung himself behind the wheel, pulling his long legs into the cab, and slammed the door. He heard gravel crunching and looked out the driver's side window to see his dad walking back to the garden center.

Whatever.

Joel turned the ignition key. Once, twice, three times. The old engine finally turned over and sputtered before settling into a chug-like rumble.

Joel slammed his hand against the steering wheel.

His dad thought he'd done Joel so many freaking favors. Like buying this pickup. "I bought you a truck, Joel," his dad often said to him when Joel was complaining about not getting something he wanted. *So what?* It was a twenty-year-old pickup with standard transmission! *Thanks for small favors, dude,* Joel thought.

Joel slapped the gear shift into reverse. He ground the gears and the truck shot backward. He could hear gravel flying under the pickup's chassis. He hoped he was leaving big furrows in his dad's precious—"the gravel needs to be kept smooth and even"—parking lot. It would serve the jackass right.

Joel ground the gears again as he shifted into first. He pressed hard on the accelerator and the engine whined, protesting the excessive speed in low gear. Joel quickly shifted through second and third as he kept accelerating. He exited the parking lot at 45 mph in third gear. Gravel was still flying; he heard it ping off the D'Agostino's sign at the front edge of the parking lot. His tires squealed as he careened out into the road. Someone honked, but he didn't even look behind him to see why. He just put the accelerator to the floor and took the truck up to over 60 mph as quickly as the old geezer of a vehicle would allow.

Another car honked. Someone shouted. Joel didn't care.

D'Agostino's was just outside the so-called downtown—a pathetic scraggly collection of dying businesses scattered over several semi-abandoned blocks. The garden center/nursery complex was on the "main" road—a narrow two-lane, pothole-filled strip of pavement that eventually led to a state highway. Although it was the main road, the speed limit was only 30 mph. Stupid slow.

The D'Agostino family house was just three miles from the nursery. Joel liked to see how fast he could drive the short distance.

Today, he couldn't get home fast enough. He needed to get back to his room and get on his drum pads. He wanted to pound out his frustration. If he could have gone to his buddy Zach's place to play drums for real, he would have, but Zach and his family weren't home today—some kind of family thing. Zach's dad didn't want Joel or the other members of the band coming over when no one was there.

Joel took the turn off the main road so fast that his tires squealed again. He grinned and accelerated onto the straightaway that ran west of the main street. A few blocks later, he was in the heart of the "old town" residential area, the neighborhood of big gnarled trees and sloping green lawns and uppity Victorian houses where all the town "somebodies" lived—the families who had been here forever. Joel actually thought these families, which included his own, were the nobodies—the people too stupid to see that their town was a waste of space, the people too lazy or scared or stupid to leave and try life someplace else.

The thought of these immovable families, all the old ways of thinking and the endless judgments and criticisms—like those of his dad—pissed off Joel so much that his foot jammed down the accelerator even harder, and he took the next turn faster than he'd ever taken it before. He took it so fast that he went into a skid. For a couple seconds, he had no control over the vehicle. He slid around the corner, his tires jittering over the uneven pavement.

Joel let out a whoop of exhilaration. It felt great to be untethered to the rules, to what was right. It was—

The back of his truck hit something with a heavy *whump* followed by a *crack*.

Oops. It sounded like he'd taken out a mailbox.

Joel sighed and slammed on his brakes. The truck lurched to a stop, throwing him forward and back and rocking for a couple seconds as he shoved the gearshift into neutral and set the parking brake. He let the engine idle as he got out to see what he'd crunched. Not that he cared a lot, but getting in trouble didn't serve his purposes right now, especially given that his dad had fired him. He needed to suck up to someone to get a better job, and most of the someones worth sucking up to lived in this neighborhood. If he'd broken a mailbox, he should probably fix it.

Joel walked around his truck and looked down at the shoulder. He lifted his brows.

He hadn't hit a mailbox.

A three-foot-tall neon-yellow-green plastic figure vaguely shaped like a kid lay on its side in the dirt behind Joel's truck. The "kid" held a triangular orange flag that had the words KIDS AT PLAY printed in black. The color of the sign matched the orange "hat" that was molded across the top of the kid's plastic head. Across what could have been called the figure's hips, the word SLOW shined under a red reflector. Joel laughed. Heck of a lot of good the little dude had done just now. Joel hadn't even seen it, much less felt compelled to heed its stupid warning.

He noticed the plastic figure's "legs" were cracked, probably as a result of their impact with Joel's truck. No big deal. The figure would still work.

Joel started to turn away from the figure, but for some reason, its large, round black eyes and gaping empty mouth caught his attention. He paused. Goose bumps formed on his bare arms as he stared into the sightless, lifeless little face.

He shook his head and rubbed his eyes. "Whatever," Joel said aloud.

He looked around. He was alone, so he once again started to return to his truck.

And again, he stopped. This time, his attention was caught by a disgusting sludge puddle by the plastic figure's feet. What was that? It wasn't mud. It wasn't dog doo-doo. It was . . .

Joel bent over to see the sludge more clearly, and he immediately recoiled. The brownish lumpy mass looked like a dog had melted into a semiliquid ooze.

Joel took a step back and made a face. "That's gross!"

Thoroughly creeped out, Joel rotated once more to see if anyone was watching him. He didn't see a soul on the street, and all the houses either had pulled curtains or darkened windows.

Joel hurried back to his open driver's door and jumped into the truck. Putting it in gear, he popped off the brake and drove away as fast as he could without squealing the tires. He didn't want to make more sound than was necessary.

Why? Because it might wake the sleeping plastic kid?

Joel snorted at the thought. "Yeah, right," he muttered. He turned on his radio to drown out the remaining heebie-jeebies that tickled the hairs at the back of his neck.

Joel's mom was waiting for him when he pulled his pickup into the driveway. She stood on the covered, wraparound porch, hands buried in the pockets of her high-waisted mom jeans. Even from thirty feet away, Joel could see her furrowed brows and her compressed lips. She was obviously pissed about something. Great.

He was tempted to take off again, but he was still feeling weird because of the plastic kid-thing. He wanted to go up to his room and shut out the world.

To do that, he'd have to get past his mom.

Joel was an only child, and as such, he always figured he should be appropriately spoiled and coddled. His best friend, Wes, was also an only child, and Wes got whatever he wanted whenever he wanted it. Joel, however, had parents who were "committed" to making sure he wasn't spoiled. Over the years he'd tried to manipulate them into getting him what he wanted, but he'd given up at some point.

"You have to work for what you get in life, Joel," his parents were always telling him. "If we give you everything, you won't know how to make your way in the world."

"I'd figure it out," he told them. "Why not give me a few easy years before I get to the hard ones?"

They didn't find his reasoning persuasive or his humor amusing.

Unlike Wes's parents, who told him it was okay when he made Cs and Ds in school, Joel's parents not only lamented his poor grades, they punished him for them. His truck was a perfect example of that.

When Joel had gotten to high school, his dad told him that he'd buy Joel a new truck when Joel got his license, provided he got good grades. For every semester he got bad grades, the truck he received would be a year older. Joel tried to get good grades for a semester, but it was too much work. It cut into his music-playing and hanging-out time. So, he did the math and figured a five-year-old truck wasn't such a bad thing; he gave up trying to get decent grades. When it came time for him to get his truck, his dad told Joel how disappointed he was in Joel's school performance. Joel proudly told his dad his reasoning for being lazy, which turned out to be a bad move. His dad was so angry that he punished Joel for his "impertinence" by taking off another fifteen years from the new truck. That was how Joel ended up with a twenty-year-old truck.

"You should be glad your dad bought you a truck at all," Joel's mother had said when he complained about it to her.

She always took his dad's side. "Your father is a wonderful man, a great father. He does his best for this family," she'd said more times than Joel wanted to remember.

Now he could tell by his mother's angry scowl that getting past her wasn't going to be easy. He decided to try acting innocent and clueless and see what that got him.

He got out of his truck and waved at his mom casually. "Hey, Mom."

"Don't you *hey, Mom* me," she snapped. "Your father called."

Joel sighed and loped toward his mother. He made sure he kept his shoulders back, his head high, and his stroll in its usually confident swagger. Marianna, the prettiest girl in his class, lived across the street. Her bedroom window looked out over the road. She'd never given him the time of day, but he figured there was always hope. After all, he made jeans and black T-shirts look hot. All the other girls thought so. They didn't seem to mind that he wasn't romantic or gentlemanly or any of that crap. He got dates whenever he wanted them. Marianna, though, was one date he couldn't get.

"Your charm is like plastic wrap, Joel," she'd said to him once.

"What's that supposed to mean?" he'd asked.

"It's thin, and because it's see-through, it doesn't cover up what a jerk you are."

Joel flicked a glance at Marianna's window as he walked toward his mother. If she was watching, the only two women he wanted to impress were seeing him at a low point. That sucked.

Joel stepped up onto the porch and looked in his mom's dark eyes.

Joel loved his mother, but she could be intimidating. She was a tall woman with a sturdy body, and she always wore no-nonsense clothes—usually dark slacks or high-waisted jeans and bright-colored blouses (today's was magenta). Her features were kind of large for her face. She actually could have passed for a man if she hadn't worn her hair long. But she commanded attention. He couldn't look away from her when she was mad.

"Dad was in a mood," Joel tried.

"Cut it out, Joel. You know darn well you've pushed your dad beyond the limits any parent should have to endure. You show up late to work, do as little as possible while you're there, and you leave early. He was going to let it slide until you went off to college, but then you announced that you weren't *going* to college . . . not that you could get in with your grades. At that point, your dad figured you'd need the money, so he kept you on, in spite of the fact that you're going to break his heart and go join a crazy rock band or whatever it is you plan to do. But even he has his breaking point."

Joel looked at his feet. "I'm sorry, Mom." He tilted his

head and gave her the sideways glance that always used to make her melt.

She blew out air. "You're a good-looking boy, Joel. I'll give you that. But looks won't get you everything. You need a little personality to go with them. And right now, yours needs a lot of work."

Joel shrugged. "I'm going up to my room."

His mom opened her mouth, then closed it and made a shooing motion with her hand. "Fine. Go."

Joel brushed past her and stomped into his house. He heard her sigh behind him as he tracked dirt across the gray-tiled entryway. Served her right.

He was kind of hungry and wanted a snack, but more than that, he wanted to be alone. He ran up the wide staircase to the second floor, strode down the hall, and went into his room. Slamming the door, he started for the drumsticks but instead grabbed his acoustic guitar from its stand in the corner of the room. He flopped on the bed with it.

Curling his fingers over the frets, Joel concentrated on the latest set of chords he was trying to master. They were barre chords, which he'd always had trouble with. Getting the strength in his fingers necessary to hold down all the strings on the fret at once took hundreds of hours of practice, and even now, after years of playing, he struggled with some of the less common chords. He had to learn them, though. He didn't want the music he was writing to be ordinary; he wasn't going to use the usual, easy chords or the standard chord progressions. He wanted to create music that pushed boundaries.

Boundaries.

That was his whole problem. He was locked in by so many rules. They made him crazy, so crazy that he felt like he was a walking ball of anger all the time. He didn't mean to be, but he couldn't seem to help himself. He felt like a tiger trapped in a cage, a tiger so frustrated that it couldn't help but roar at everyone.

Joel went through his new chords twice; then he started combining them with complex picking. The mix sounded supercool. Joel grinned as a new song, about breaking boundaries, began to form in his head.

But the fledgling melody was silenced when Joel's mother threw open his bedroom door. Joel's fingers froze on the guitar.

Joel's mom walked over to his dresser and put clean socks in a drawer. "That sounded interesting," she said.

Joel frowned. "Interesting" wasn't what he was going for. But he wasn't going to say anything. He never tried to explain his music to his parents. It wasn't for them to understand. It was for him, and for the fans he'd eventually have when he was able to leave this town and play someplace where he'd be appreciated.

Joel's mom flicked a look from Joel to the plush-backed stool that sat in the corner with his instruments. She put her hands on her hips. "Why did we bother getting you that stool if you're going to slouch on your bed when you play your guitar?" She shook her head and left his room, muttering to herself.

As soon as she closed the bedroom door, Joel threw a pillow at it. "Why did we bother?" he mimicked her.

Why did we bother? was one of his mom's favorite lines. This line applied to anything she or Joel's dad did that she thought Joel should appreciate more.

For instance, she loved to ask, "Why did we bother getting you nice clothes if you're not going to take care of them?" and "Why did we bother getting you a tutor if you're not going to show up for your lessons?"

He never answered her when she asked these questions, but if he had, he'd have said something like "Who asked for nice clothes? Jeans and T-shirts are fine." And "When did I *ask* for a tutor?"

If he'd thought he could get away with it, he'd have the most to say in answer to her question about his room: "Why did we bother decorating your room if you were going to trash it?"

Well, did Joel *ask* her to bring in a professional decorator to coordinate just the right beige-and-blue-striped curtains to go with the dark blue walls in his room? Did he *ask* for the custom oak study center—desk and credenza attached to built-in filing cabinets and shelves—and the matching chest of drawers and nightstand and dresser? Did he care about the imported Turkish rug or the framed art prints of rare plants? Did he need a state-of-the-art brushed-steel ceiling fan and light? Did stuff like thread count and pillow shapes matter to him? Why did he need six decorative pillows anyway? When his room was straightened up the way his mom liked it—which only happened when either she or the housekeeper did it—the damn pillows took up most of his queen-size bed.

All Joel had ever wanted for his room was enough space for his drum set and guitars, a professional sound board, and soundproofing. Instead, he got a room full of hoity-toity men's club–looking furniture and decorative crap, which forced him to cram his instruments—the only thing he *did* care about—into a corner. And the lack of soundproofing made it really hard to practice. His parents always were either making comments on music he wanted to keep to himself or they were yelling at him to keep it down.

The problem with Joel's mom and dad was that they'd decided what was right for him, and they got mad at him for having a different idea. He never got to choose for himself. Over the years, this had made him so resentful that he could no longer appreciate even the rare things they did that he actually liked.

Joel gritted his teeth and started playing his guitar again. He sang softly along. "Boundaries stealing choice from me—shoving, forcing, making me be not me." He stopped. That was lame.

Joel sighed and laid back on his pillows, cradling his silent guitar.

If only I could leave now, he thought.

His dad had told him that if he didn't graduate from high school, Joel would never receive another penny from his dad—not now, not if he got in trouble, not even after his dad was dead. Joel believed him.

At the moment, he'd have been willing to give up any of that money just to get away, but he didn't have enough saved to make the trip, or to get his own place. He needed to stay at home a little longer. And now he had to find a new job . . . unless he could find a way to make his dad forgive him. Maybe he could convince his dad to take him back.

Joel thought about that for a while. Which was worse? Groveling to his dad or going out and trying to find a different job? Both choices sucked, but he finally decided apologizing would be less time-consuming than job hunting.

By putting on what he thought was an award-worthy acting performance over a dinner of roast beef, red potatoes, and peas, Joel was able to persuade his dad to let him keep working until the end of the school year. Joel had been all "I'm really sorry I've been acting like a jerk." And he'd thrown in a bunch of stuff like "I've been doing a lot of thinking, and I get that I need to make some changes," and "I think I've been taking things for granted, and I'm not going to do that anymore."

He thought his blah, blah, blah lies had gone well with the blah meal. Joel's mom was into cooking "simple food." She actually took classes on how to put together meals with the fewest ingredients possible. He wished she didn't have time for classes like that—the food was terribly bland—but she only had a part-time, work-at-home hobby job writing knitting patterns and selling them online. This gave her too much time to "discover" new things like "cooking simply."

For the last two years, nothing they ate had any flavor. Last Christmas, he'd tried to fix that by spending some of his own money to buy a spice rack filled with thirty spices for his mom. She'd ended up giving away all but a dozen of the spices. "What use do I have for ginger and coriander?" she'd said as she'd put them in a bag to donate to charity. And his parents wondered why he didn't do stuff for them. What was the point? It was never right anyway.

Just two more months.

The next morning, feeling pretty pleased with himself for getting his job back, Joel slouched on one of the burgundy-velveteen-covered stools in front of the aircraft-carrier-size island in his mother's restaurant-quality kitchen. For probably the 3,000th time, Joel looked from his bowl of cold cereal to the flashy stainless-steel appliances and the gleaming black granite countertops in his mother's kitchen. How did these two things make sense? About ten years before, his dad had surprised his mom with this massive kitchen remodel (instead of building Joel the soundproof music studio *he* wanted). His dad had bought all state-of-the-art this and top-quality that, and Joel still got cold cereal six mornings a week. The only time he got a hot breakfast was on Sunday mornings, before church . . . and that was only because his dad was home.

Monday through Saturday, Joel's dad left the house before dawn to get the garden center ready to open. Too often, Joel was expected to go in early with his dad. More than half the time he had the early shift, he overslept. What normal person wouldn't? It wasn't natural to wake up when it was still dark.

Joel ground his way through a second bowl of Fazbear Fazcrunch cereal, wishing the whole time it was something else—like curried eggs and bacon with hash browns. Maybe he should have gone over to Zach's house. Zach's mom always made what she called "farmhouse breakfasts."

"Glaring at your cereal isn't going to turn it into pancakes . . . or whatever you're wishing it was," Joel's mom said as she tossed a knitting magazine on the counter next to him and sat down with her cup of coffee. As usual, she was already dressed (today's slacks were black, and the blouse was emerald green) and had her hair braided and her makeup in place.

He tossed her a look. "I still don't get why we can't have eggs during the week."

"Nothing's stopping you from having eggs. You want eggs? Cook eggs." Joel's mom took a sip of her coffee and kept her gaze on her magazine.

"Just because you don't eat breakfast doesn't mean you shouldn't feed your family breakfast," Joel grumbled. "It's not fair to make me eat cereal every day because you think coffee is all a person needs in the morning."

Joel's mom put down her magazine and turned to look at him. "You have an interesting perspective, Joel," his mom said.

He frowned at her. "What's that mean?"

"You've conveniently forgotten all the days you were little, when I got up early and fixed you eggs or pancakes or waffles or oatmeal only to have you run down the stairs, late as always, and yell, 'I don't have time, Momma!

Just give me cereal.' After dumping a few dozen breakfasts down the garbage disposal, I got the message." She
pointed at his cereal box. "That's what you wanted. That's
what you get."

"Yeah, well, it sucks, and I don't think it's fair to punish
me for something I don't even remember doing."

His mom crossed her arms and raised an eyebrow at
him. "What happened to 'I get that I need to make some
changes'?" She did a pretty good impression of his voice
as she shoved the previous night's sucking-up back in his
face. She took a deep breath, then frowned and shook her
head. "You didn't bother to shower this morning, did
you? As usual."

Joel pressed his lips together. Again with the showering. His mother was obsessed with cleanliness.

"I didn't have time," he said.

"But you have *time* to sit here and grouse about the
food you're eating, which was provided to you free of
charge, by the way."

Joel wanted to say something snarky to that, but he
knew anything he said would get back to his dad. When
his dad had agreed to let him come back to work, it had
come with a warning: "You'd better keep your nose
clean. No slacking off. No backtalk."

So Joel kept his mouth shut.

His mom wrinkled her nose and picked up her coffee
and her magazine. "I think I'm going to take my coffee
up to my office and read my magazine in peace."

"Whatever," Joel muttered.

His mother stood next to the island for a moment and

stared at him. Then she sighed and left the kitchen.

Joel rolled his eyes and grimaced at the couple soggy bits of Fazcrunch that floated in his bowl. He'd already had two bowls of the stuff, and he was still hungry. He picked up the bright-red box and, putting his thumb over Freddy Fazbear's face, tried to shake a third bowl's worth from the near-empty box. A couple more cereal bits fell out, along with something small and yellow, wrapped in cellophane. Right. The toy prize inside every box.

Fishing the prize out of the milk with his spoon—and spraying the counter with milk in the process—Joel looked at the toy. Was that . . . ?

He wiped the cellophane on the napkin lying next to his cereal bowl and tore open the wrapping to see the toy more clearly. It *couldn't* be what he thought it was.

The plastic toy clattered onto the counter, and Joel flinched. It *was* what he'd thought it was.

The toy was a miniature version of the same freaky yellow plastic kid-shaped figure he'd hit with his truck yesterday. Just like that figure, the toy held an orange triangular flag that read KIDS AT PLAY. Just like that figure, the toy had SLOW printed across its hips, under a red reflector. It had the same orange hat, the black eyes, the gaping mouth. The thing was *identical* in all respects—except for size—to the plastic figure Joel had hit. Identical . . . even to the way it made him feel when he looked at it. The thing seriously weirded him out.

"That's just whacked," Joel said aloud, as if to snap himself out of it.

What were the odds? Why would anyone even *make* a toy that looked like that stupid kid figure?

Joel shivered, then flicked the stupid toy off the counter with his index finger. It hit the floor with a *clickety-click*, slid across the polished hardwood, and landed between a heat register vent and the baseboard trim in the corner of the kitchen. Joel looked at it for a couple seconds, then left the kitchen, leaving his empty bowl and the empty cereal box on the counter . . . as he always did. He figured if he had to eat cereal every day, it served his mother right to have to clean up the dregs of it.

Joel glanced at the clock over the stove. He'd better get a move on. He was going to be late for school. One more official tardy notice, and he'd have to do after-school detention. If he got detention, he couldn't work. Without work, he couldn't get the money he needed.

Life seriously sucked. Nothing you wanted came without paying for it, and when your parents wouldn't pay for the stuff you wanted, you had to get the money yourself. That meant you spent most of your life doing crap you didn't want to do, just to eventually have enough money to do something you *did* want to do, but by then you didn't have enough time to do what you wanted because you were working to pay for it.

Joel barely made it to school on time, and after school, he barely made it to work on time. Once there, he had to stay until 6:00 p.m. *exactly*. Actually, he stayed until five minutes after just to be sure his dad got the point that he wasn't "slacking."

He had to do the same thing the next day, and the next day, until finally, it was Friday.

At 6:08 p.m., Joel trudged toward his truck, muttering under his breath and kicking gravel as he went. His dad wanted Joel at work early the next morning to load up a special order for delivery. On a *Saturday* morning. That wasn't fair at all. His dad knew Joel and his friends liked practicing late on Friday nights. Joel would be wiped in the morning, and now he couldn't sleep in! The worst part was that he couldn't even complain because he'd promised not to.

But if his promise meant late evenings and early mornings, then he—

"Ow! Watch what you're doing, young man!"

Joel lifted his eyes and looked around. He groaned when his gaze landed on old Mrs. Linden.

At least ninety years old, Mrs. Linden was this bony old lady who visited the garden center at least once a week. "Gardening keeps the bones young," she said *every single time* she came to buy a new plant or a new tool. The woman repeated herself over and over and over again.

This was especially tiresome since Mrs. Linden was a talker. She rambled constantly about everything that was going on in her life, about her grown kids and their problems, about her aches and pains and doctor's appointments, and, of course, about every minuscule thing that happened in her huge garden.

"The bees have been hovering around my forsythia more than usual."

"I nearly cut a caterpillar in half when I was planting the new alyssum."

"One of the branches broke on my tam juniper."

Who the hell cared about all this stuff? Joel sure didn't. He hated listening to the old lady's cracked voice.

And on top of Mrs. Linden constantly running her mouth, she was a complainer. She found fault with something every time she came in, and his dad always bent over backward to make her happy. Joel cringed every time he had to listen to one of their exchanges, which always went something like . . .

Mrs. Linden: "Those seeds didn't sprout on schedule, Steven."

Dad: "I'm so sorry, Mrs. Linden. Here's a new packet of them. On the house."

Or this:

Mrs. Linden: "My hyacinths aren't as rich in color as I had hoped they'd be, Steven. I don't believe the fertilizer is doing its job."

Dad: "I'm so sorry, Mrs. Linden. How about I give you a small bottle of another type of fertilizer for you to try, no charge?"

After witnessing this several times, Joel finally asked his dad, "Why does she bother coming here all the time if our stuff sucks so bad?"

His dad smiled and shook his head. "It's just her way. She buys much more than I give to her."

Now Mrs. Linden was leveling her gray-eyed squinty stare at Joel. "You do realize that your casual gravel kicking just resulted in a divot in my fender," Mrs. Linden said, pointing at a microscopic speck in the pale blue paint of her ancient Ford LTD. The thing was a boat on wheels.

Joel opened his mouth to tell her where to stick her divot, but out of the corner of his eye, he saw his dad step out of the garden center. Joel and Mrs. Linden were close enough to his dad that his dad could hear what they said. Joel blew out air and bent over to brush his thumb over the speck. Thankfully, the speck was dirt, not a "divot."

"I'm very sorry, Mrs. Linden," he said, practically choking on every word. "I shouldn't have been so careless. But it's just a bit of dirt, not a divot. How about if I wash your car for you tomorrow after I get off work?"

Mrs. Linden beamed. "That would be lovely, young man." She shuffled over to Joel's dad. "A nice boy you have there."

Joel's dad quirked his lips but nodded. Joel rolled his eyes and dashed to his truck as soon as Mrs. Linden took another step toward his dad. Jumping into the cab, he stuck his key in the ignition and commanded, "Start!" Amazingly, it did so on the first try.

Joel put the truck in gear, and because he could almost literally feel his dad's gaze on him, he backed up slowly. He ever-so-carefully turned the wheels to head out of the parking area. He was toeing the line perfectly today, so much so that it was the first thing he said to Zach when he pulled up next to Zach's family's old barn.

Zach was outside, at the corner of the barn, putting seeds in the bird feeder when Joel arrived. Joel could see Zach had already spread out fresh hay for the goats. One of the goats, Missy, a tan-colored nanny who would eat your clothes if you didn't watch her, was already chowing down. The air smelled similar to the way the nursery smelled: it reeked of dirt and manure with just a hint of sweetness—that came from the honeysuckle growing against the faded and warped boards along the barn's south wall.

"Dude," Joel called as he got out of his truck, "I'm toeing the line today. How about you?"

Zach turned and laughed. "Nah. I'm stomping all over the lines."

Joel laughed and reached through the cab of his truck and grabbed the handle of his battered guitar case.

"Everyone here?" he asked Zach.

Zach shook his head, and his long, straw-colored hair flipped across his face. He brushed it aside with a large hand.

Zach was a big guy, even taller than Joel. He was the kind of dude you didn't want to cross. The center on the high school football team, Zach's muscle mass didn't come from working out. It came from working on his parents' farm. He was incredibly strong. He was also a great musician. He didn't look like it because he was big, tanned, and had rough features, but Zach could play the piano and keyboard with more heart than anyone Joel had ever heard.

Zach closed the lid on the bird feeder. "Evan's girlfriend had a thing. He'll be here in an hour."

"We don't need him. I can sing lead until he gets here."

"Figured."

"Pizza come yet?" Joel asked. "I'm starved."

"Wes talked me into waiting to order, so it wouldn't be cold when Evan got here." Zach headed into the barn, and Joel followed him.

"Wes!" Joel shouted at his short, curly-haired dolt of a friend. "What were you thinking, dude? I need food!"

"It's not all about you, Joel," Wes said.

"Stick it in your ear." Joel set his case on a bale of hay and took out his guitar. He crossed to one of the amps set up at the back of the barn, plugged the guitar in, and left it leaning against a couple spare tires stacked along the wall. He didn't play guitar in the group that often. Mostly, he was the drummer. Sometimes, though, he and Evan switched out. Evan was a passable drummer, and he could keep the beat when Joel really wanted to be on the guitar.

Joel watched Wes concentrate on a riff he was working on, his dark brown hair flopping over his pale face.

"Sick," Joel said when Wes stopped playing.

Zach sat down at the keyboard. "We starting?"

Joel took his seat behind the drum set. He and Wes followed Zach's lead into the song they'd been practicing the night before. The barn had surprisingly good acoustics, and Joel was lost in the music within seconds of beating the skins.

Evan arrived around the time the pizza arrived, and after they all stuffed themselves on pepperoni and pepperoncini pizza, they returned to playing. They jammed until Joel glanced at his watch just after midnight.

"I gotta quit early tonight," he said. "My freaking dad is forcing me to get up before dawn to work."

Wes set down his guitar and stretched. "Hey, be glad you have that job. I'd kill to work for someone like your dad."

Joel grimaced. "You don't know what you're talking about. My dad's a slave driver."

"You've never flipped burgers at BJ's. Now, *that guy* is a slave driver!" Wes groaned. "Minimum wage for working over a dirty, hot grill, getting yelled at all the time because you're not doing it fast enough."

"At least you don't have to shovel manure," Joel said.

Zach laughed. "I think you're shoveling some yourself, Joel." He got up from the keyboard and shook his head. "You've got a great life, dude, and instead of appreciating it, you're always grousing about it. You're in such a hurry to leave it behind."

Joel frowned at his friend. "You want to get into the music scene, too. You said you *couldn't wait* for us to go out on our own."

"Yeah, but that's a figure of speech. I'm looking forward to it, but I also can appreciate what I have now. I just think sometimes your anger blinds you to what's good is all."

"What the hell do you know about it?" Joel snapped.

Zach held up his hands in surrender. "Dude. Just sayin' . . . if you slow down in life, you can enjoy the scenery on the way to where you want to be."

Joel snorted. "What are you? Some kind of guru?"

When Zach just smiled and shrugged, Joel slammed his guitar into its case and stomped out of the barn. Joel was grinding his teeth when he got into his truck under a star-filled sky and a quarter moon. Where did Zach get off telling Joel what to do? Joel got enough of that from his parents.

"See you guys tomorrow night!" Evan called as he and Wes headed toward their own vehicles.

Joel grudgingly waved at his friends, pulled out, and headed toward the gates of Zach's family's farm. He could see Evan's headlights behind him. Evan drove an old red sports car that had bug-eyed headlights set close together. Tall and lanky, Evan barely fit in the thing, but he loved it—inherited it from his grandpa. Too bad Joel didn't have a grandpa. His parents' parents were all dead . . . long dead. He hadn't inherited squat from any of them. How was that fair?

Behind Evan's little car, Wes's jacked-up truck shot light over the top of Evan's car and in through Joel's rear window. The searing light reflected into his eyes from the rearview mirror, pissing him off—he should have a big truck like Wes's, instead of this old piece of garbage he was driving. He shoved his foot down on the accelerator in anger, and as he shot through the gates of the farm, he fishtailed onto the country road and punched it back toward town.

Rattling just enough to piss him off even more, Joel's truck attempted to reach 80 mph on the straight stretch of narrow road that ran along the edge of the farm on one side and an old forest on the other side. If Evan or Wes had been coming this way, too, Joel was sure they could have caught up to him in a nanosecond and blown him off the road. Thankfully, though, they lived on the other side of town, and they took a different route home.

Lowering the passenger side window so he could feel air rushing through the cab, Joel let out a shout. Whether it was a shout of rage or a shout of glee, he couldn't have said. His emotions were a mess. He hated his truck, but he was loving the feel of its 435-horsepower engine rumbling under his control.

The country road leading back to civilization came to a fork in the road near town. One branch of the Y led to more farms spreading out into the valley. The other led abruptly into one of the town's outlying subdivisions, an expanse of twenty-year-old ramblers that all looked alike and sat too close together. Joel hated the subdivision, but even though the speed limit in the area was just 25 mph, cutting through it got him home faster, and he needed to get back and catch some sleep if he was going to make it to work before dawn.

Joel slowed as he downshifted for the turn into the subdivision, but he didn't slow enough. Just as he had earlier in the week, he slid around the corner out of control. Fighting to keep the truck on the road because he sure as heck didn't want to go in the deep ditch he knew ran along the shoulder here, Joel cursed at himself for being so reckless. He knew better than to take the corner at this speed.

At one point, he felt the tires come off the road, and for a split second, he thought the truck was going to flip. His heart stopped beating for an instant. But then the truck settled, even though it was still in a skid.

Joel let the truck have its way with the asphalt, and he even began enjoying the adrenaline rush of the slide. He enjoyed it, that is, until he saw the child caught in his headlights.

A child?

What in the hell was a kid doing out after midnight?

As soon as he saw the kid, Joel jammed his foot on his brakes. He didn't even downshift. He just hit the brakes. The truck bucked, but it didn't slow fast enough. The front bumper slammed into the child with a *thud* that seemed to reverberate through the truck and right into Joel's body.

As soon as he heard the impact, Joel wanted to squeeze his eyes shut and pretend he was someplace else, but he couldn't. It was like his gaze was tied by a string to the trajectory of the child's body as it flew up and out, away from the truck and then disappeared off the road. He assumed they landed in the deep ditch just off the pavement.

The truck lurched to a stop, and because Joel hadn't depressed the clutch, the engine died. A few clicks sounded from under the hood, and Joel's panting breath filled the cab. Outside, crickets chirruped. In the distance, a dog barked.

Joel forced himself to quiet his breathing. He needed to listen. Was there any sound coming from the ditch? Was the kid . . . ?

Joel closed his eyes tight, but that didn't do anything to make what had just happened go away. As soon as his lids came down, his mind replayed the impact of his truck against the kid . . . in slow motion. Joel was able to see details he'd missed when it had happened in real time.

In this slo-mo replay, Joel was able to see that the kid's body was small. The kid couldn't have been more than six or seven, maybe. And what was it? A boy or a girl? It was impossible to tell. The kid was wearing dark pants, maybe jeans, and a dark jacket. He . . . she? Joel decided to stick with *it*. Thinking *it* didn't feel as bad as *he* or *she*.

Again, what in the hell was a kid doing out at this hour?

Joel sat behind the wheel and thought about the body his truck had just tossed into the ditch. He should get out and check on it. Shouldn't he? Of course he should.

But he couldn't. He just absolutely couldn't. The very thought of trying to get out of his truck made him start to shake. No, that wasn't true. He already *was* shaking. But the idea of getting out of the truck made him shake even more intensely.

It suddenly occurred to Joel that he should check and see if anyone was watching. Had anyone witnessed what he'd just done?

The entry to the subdivision was flanked with two big

stone monument-like signs that announced the sub-division's name—Glenwood Fields. A decorative area filled with seasonal flowers—daffodils now—surrounded the signs. The first houses on the street were well beyond the decorative area. This meant no houses looked directly out at the corner. And even the nearest houses were dark. No one seemed to be up . . . except the crazy kid in the middle of the road.

Joel realized he was gripping the steering wheel so tightly that his palms were starting to hurt. He let go of it and stretched his hands.

"What are you going to do, dude?" he asked himself out loud.

His stomach felt heavy; the pizza he'd eaten was gurgling around and threatening to climb back up into his throat. He pressed a hand to his stomach.

What should he do?

For some reason, he glanced in his review mirror. And his decision was made for him.

Headlights were coming down the country road, heading toward the corner. No way was he going to be caught sitting here.

His legs feeling weak and rubbery, Joel managed to position his feet on the clutch pedal and the brake pedal. With a trembling hand, Joel reached for the key and turned the ignition. To his surprise, it started immediately.

Joel put his hands at two o'clock and ten o'clock on the steering wheel and eased out the clutch as he gently accelerated. As soon as the truck was rolling, he sped up, and in spite of what had just happened, he raced home at double the posted speed limit the whole way.

Joel should have fallen asleep the second he threw himself on his bed. He was beyond tired.

Apparently, however, he was so far beyond tired that he'd circled back around to wide-awake. His eyes just wouldn't close. It was like they were taped open or something.

Most Friday and Saturday nights, because of the long days and late nights playing music, Joel went to sleep so fast that he'd wake up the next morning on top of his covers in the exact same position as when he fell into his bed. This drove his mom crazy, usually triggering one of her "why did we bother" lines: "Why did we bother getting you nice sheets and blankets when you're just going to sleep on top of them?"

Joel turned over for the third time since he'd flopped in his bed. It didn't do any good. He was still wide-awake. No matter how much Joel squirmed around in his bed or scrunched and re-scrunched his pillow to get his body in a comfortable position, his eyes remained open, staring at the shadows in his overstuffed room. But no, his eyes weren't staring at the shadows. That was the problem. His eyes apparently were still back at the entrance to Glenwood Fields, and they were stuck in a time loop there, watching the little kid get flung into the ditch over and over and over.

Joel groaned and wiped his eyes with the back of his knuckles, as if he could erase his inner film loop by scrubbing it away. It didn't work. Not only was the kid still flying through the air in Joel's mind, now Joel's eyeballs felt like they'd rolled in gravel and been stuck back in his head. His eyes felt scratchy, and they stung.

Joel sat up and turned on the wrought-iron lamp on his nightstand. He rubbed his eyes again, and he put his head in his hands. He breathed in and out a few times and squared his shoulders. He should go back.

He really should.

The kid could be alive, just hurt and unable to get out of the ditch. It wasn't terribly cold out tonight, but it was still chilly. The kid had been wearing that dark jacket—dumb kid—so it wasn't going to freeze to death or anything. But what if it was bleeding? Joel had to check on the kid.

He stood. He tried to take a step toward the door of his room, but he couldn't. His sense of self-preservation wouldn't let him.

Even though his morals wanted him to go do the right thing, his survival instinct had a different opinion. It was laying out the facts:

The second Joel went back to check on the kid, he was committing himself to deep trouble. Even if he could pretend that he hadn't left the scene of the accident, the fact that he knew the kid was in the ditch would be an admission of guilt that he'd hit the kid. His skid marks would prove he was going too fast as he went around that corner. He'd be charged with reckless driving at minimum. And if the kid was dead . . .

Joel started breathing fast, so he sat back down. He hugged himself and rocked back and forth. He knew he was acting like a little kid himself, but he didn't care. He was on the verge of a panic attack.

If the kid was dead and Joel admitted that he was the one who hit the kid, Joel would go to jail. No going to LA to break into the music scene. No being free to live his life. If he thought working for a living was its own kind of prison, there was no way he would last long in an actual prison.

Joel quickly reached out and turned off his lamp. He got under the covers and pulled them up to his chin. With great determination, he was able to force his eyes closed. He was doing his best to imitate a normal person getting ready to sleep instead of a guilty person too spun up to sleep.

Joel's eyes opened again. That was the problem. He was guilty of a crime, and he knew it. He'd hit a kid, and he'd fled the scene. He couldn't justify what he'd done the way he could justify leaving work a few minutes early or getting bad grades or not taking as many showers as his mom wanted him to take. There was no "Hey, that's just who I am" defense for what he'd done. It was *wrong*. No one would argue differently.

Right now, the kid Joel hit could be dying because no one—except Joel—knew the kid was in the ditch. It was wrong . . . no, it was bordering on downright despicable, to leave the kid there.

But face it, that's what Joel was going to do. He had to accept it. He wasn't about to get out of bed and go check on the kid and risk getting arrested for what he'd done. He just wasn't.

Besides, if the kid was alive, maybe he could get out on his own. Maybe someone else would find him.

And if he was dead, what did it matter?

When the overhead light in Joel's room went on, it almost literally reached into Joel's bed, scooped him up, and tossed him across the room. The brightness was so shocking that Joel catapulted from his bed and didn't realize what was going on until he was stumbling through a pile of discarded smelly T-shirts.

"Rise and shine," his mom said.

What the—?

Joel shook his head and blinked, squinting against the brain-searing light that assaulted his eyes. Past sleep-crusted eyelids, he could see his mother standing in the doorway of his room. Her hair was in the topknot she put it in for sleep, and she was wrapped in her red terry-cloth robe.

"Your dad's in the shower," his mom said. "He'll be ready to go in fifteen minutes. I didn't hear your alarm go off, so I figured I should wake you. You'd better get ready."

Joel moaned and began shuffling toward his bathroom. He had to pee, and he needed to do something about the cotton that must have been stuffed into his head while he slept.

"Joel?" his mother said.

He turned and frowned at her. "What? I'm up."

"I can see that. But move a little faster, would you?"

Joel grimaced and returned to shuffling. He was

almost to the bathroom. What did she want him to do? Leap to the toilet in a single bound?

"Joel?"

He whirled and glared at her. "What?"

She sighed. "Take a shower. You stink."

Joel turned away from her without answering. He went into his bathroom and shut the door.

Hoping his mother would be gone when he came out of the bathroom, Joel peed, splashed water on his face, and pulled on the jeans and T-shirt he'd left lying on the floor the night before. What was the point in showering and putting on clean clothes when he was going to be sweaty within the first half hour of working at the nursery?

Joel faced himself in the mirror. Man, he looked like crap. His usually thick, wavy hair was limp. He looked pale. His eyes were bloodshot. What was wrong with—

Oh yeah. That.

Apparently, sometime during the night, Joel had managed the miracle of finding sleep. And when he went to sleep, he'd also had another miracle—he'd forgotten what he'd done.

But now he'd remembered.

Joel dropped the toilet seat lid and sat down. He took several deep breaths.

His mind started to review what he'd done, but he stopped it. "No!" he snapped. He wasn't doing the replay again today.

It was bad enough he had to get up before 5:00 a.m. to work. He wasn't going to add a guilt trip on top of it.

It might not be too late, his conscience whispered to him. *You could go help the kid.*

He stood up and charged out of the bathroom. He still wore the socks he had on the night before, and he didn't bother changing them. Instead, he stuffed his feet into the dirty shoes he'd kicked off before he'd dropped into his bed. He unearthed one of his D'Agostino Garden Center baseball caps from under a pile of dirty socks and jammed it on his head. He grabbed his wallet and his keys from the pile of sheet music on his desk, and he left his room.

He ran into his dad in the hallway. "Good. You're ready," his dad said.

Joel grunted, then said, "Let's do this."

He followed his dad down the hall, his shoes sinking into the plush gray carpet and his nostrils twitching in reaction to his dad's powerful, musky cologne. He kept his gaze focused on his dad's precisely trimmed graying black hair and the farmer's-tanned skin on the back of his neck.

Joel kept his brain turned off.

His dad trotted down the stairs and headed into the kitchen. Joel followed.

His mom stood at the counter, still in her robe. She appeared to be watching her coffee brew. The kitchen was filled with the smell of it.

Joel's dad stopped to kiss his wife. Joel ignored his parents and went through the utility room and out into the garage. He was getting into his truck when his dad stepped into the garage and pressed the garage door opener.

"Why don't we head in together this morning?" Joel's dad asked. "We can stop and get donuts on the way."

Joel inwardly cringed, but he was too distracted by what he'd done the night before to argue. He shrugged. "Whatever." He closed his truck door and got into his dad's truck.

His dad grinned and slid in behind the wheel.

"Three dozen donuts coming up," his dad said. "One dozen plain glazed. One dozen chocolate covered. One dozen jelly-filled."

Joel glanced at his dad and ignored the urge to roll his eyes. It sounded like his dad was giving his order, and they were still in the garage.

"Raspberry jelly, of course," his dad continued.

"What else?" Joel said, just to say something. He couldn't have cared less about the donuts.

His mind was still stuck in the loop of the kid going into the ditch. Over and over and over. Joel clenched his fists.

Should he tell his dad what he did so they could go check on the kid?

His dad started his practically new truck with a push of a button and backed down the driveway. He pulled away from the house and accelerated.

Joel pressed his lips together and took a deep breath. He was clearly losing it. There was no way he was going to tell his dad he'd hit a kid! Why did he even think that? Joel forced himself to look out at the dark street in front of them. He shoved aside the image of the kid in the ditch.

Joel usually cut through Glenwood Fields to get to

Sally's. The café was just outside town, on the opposite end from the garden center. Going through downtown was slower because of the stoplights. Joel hated stoplights. Thankfully, though, his dad loved driving through downtown, so Joel didn't have to face Glenwood Fields.

"Consistency is the key to a good life, Joel," his dad said as he turned onto Main Street. "Same donuts. Same customers. Same good results."

Joel raised an eyebrow at his dad. He so wanted to tell his dad how full of it he was, but instead he turned and looked out the window. As soon as he looked, he was sorry he did . . . because he glimpsed one of those plastic Kids at Play figures sitting at the edge of the sidewalk.

Has that always been there? Joel frowned and turned to look back at it.

The yellowish kid-shaped figure squatted next to a rosebush in front of the last house before the business section of town began. Joel was pretty sure he'd never seen one of those plastic things next to that rosebush.

The truck came to a stop, and Joel looked ahead through the windshield. They were at the first of four stoplights in the tiny downtown area. The street was deserted because it was still dark out. None of the businesses were open.

The street lights and lit-up window displays along the sidewalk cast yellow and pale white glows out onto the empty pavement. A flash of irritation lit up in Joel's mind. How dumb was it that they were sitting here, idling at a stoplight when there wasn't anyone else around?

Joel shifted in his seat. It was making him nuts sitting here in this truck. He needed to get to the nursery so he could get to work. For once, he looked forward to it. It would take his mind off . . .

Joel groaned.

"You do realize LA has nothing but traffic jams and stoplights?" his dad said.

"Huh?" Joel said.

"I can feel your impatience, son," his dad said. "I know you hate stoplights. I was just reminding you that there will be a lot of them where you plan to go."

Joel didn't want to talk about stoplights. "That's different."

"A stoplight is a stoplight is a stoplight," his dad said. "I've always kind of liked stoplights. Gives you a breather, a chance to look around and notice things." Joel's dad glanced toward the right side of the road. He grinned and pointed. "See, like that right there. See that pink dress in the window of Lovely Ladies?"

The light turned green, and Joel's dad didn't press on the accelerator. Joel turned and looked in the direction his dad was pointing. He nodded when he saw a frilly pink dress.

"Lori Unger had a dress like that when we were in fifth grade. Boy, did I have a crush on her!" Joel's dad finally went through the intersection.

Joel once again turned to look out the window, but his vision was blurring the storefronts, the lights, and the sidewalk. Instead of seeing downtown, he was seeing the kid in the ditch.

It took a couple more minutes to get through the other stoplights. During that time, Joel's dad started rambling about some new kind of fertilizer he wanted to stock. Joel couldn't do anything but grunt in response because just before the last stoplight, he'd spotted yet another one of the Kids at Play plastic figures. This one he was *sure* he'd never seen before. It sat at the corner of Main and Fifth, next to the old phone booth by the gas station. There was no way one of those figures had been there a couple days ago, when Joel stopped to get gas. No way.

Joel stared at the thing, and he could have sworn it was looking back at him accusingly. But that wasn't possible. Right?

After what felt like an eternity, Joel's dad finally pulled into Sally's nearly empty parking lot. It was a few minutes before five.

He drove around to the back of the log cabin–style building. Sally's didn't open until six, but she started making donuts and sweet rolls in the middle of the night. Joel's dad had a standing order with Sally for three dozen donuts every Saturday morning. Joel never saw the point of the donuts, but his dad swore it brought more people into the garden center on Saturdays.

Joel's dad stopped his truck near the café's back door. "Can you run in and get the donuts?" he asked Joel.

"Sure." Joel threw open the passenger door eagerly. He needed to be moving, not sitting still, thinking.

It was still completely dark outside. The sun wasn't even debating getting up yet. It was full-on asleep behind the mountains in the distance. The quarter moon was still lingering in the sky, shining its weak light down on the craggy outlines of the mountains' peaks.

Joel had no trouble seeing, though. A glaring spotlight on a pole next to Sally's threw its illumination down over the back door.

Even without the light, Joel could have found his way. The aromas of frying oil, sugar, cinnamon, and chocolate wafted out from the partially open doorway.

Joel grasped the door's rough handle and pulled it open. "Sally?" he called.

She didn't answer, but he stepped inside. The door opened into the huge kitchen that ran along the back side of the building. Sally was always in that kitchen this time of morning.

But today, she wasn't here.

Joel stopped and looked around. He cocked his head and listened.

Past the sounds of sizzling oil and the hum of the walk-in refrigerator, he heard a woman talking. The words were muted, but it sounded like Sally. She had a deep, distinctive gravelly voice.

Joel hesitated, looking around to see if the donuts might just be ready for him to take. Sometimes they were, and he knew his dad paid monthly, so all Joel had to do was pick them up. However, no donut boxes sat on the counter. In fact, very little was on the counters. A mixing bowl was filled with some kind of batter. A couple pans of cinnamon rolls were sitting near the oven. But where were all the cooling racks filled with donuts?

Joel took a step toward the voice he could still hear. He called Sally's name again.

The voice stopped talking. A scrape preceded a tapping sound, and Sally stepped into the kitchen from a hallway at the far end of it. "Oh, Joel. It's you. Sorry. I'm behind." Sally wiped her eyes and bustled toward Joel.

A plump woman with hair dyed even blacker than Joel's was naturally, Sally was probably in her seventies by now. Her face was lined, but it was always cheerful . . . except for today.

Joel frowned at Sally's smudged mascara, her red eyes, and her compressed lips. "Um, are you okay?" he asked.

He didn't really care how she was, but he figured he should say something. She was obviously not acting normally.

"Oh, Joel, no. I'm not okay." Sally perched on a stool near the long marble counter where she rolled dough. Joel was used to seeing that counter filled with cut-out donuts ready for the fryer.

Sally looked at the counter as if she was seeing what was usually there, too. "I'm so behind. When I got the news, I just stopped baking. I couldn't even think. I've been on the phone calling people who might have seen him. Talking to Chief Montgomery. He's taking it seriously, thank God."

Joel had no idea what Sally was talking about. "I'm sorry?" he said. "What news?"

As soon as he asked, he knew the answer.

This was a small town. It was unlikely there was some

upsetting news that had nothing to do with a child who'd gotten hit by a truck the night before.

Or maybe that wasn't true. Maybe Sally's upset had nothing to do with what Joel had done. His mother, even his friends, were always telling him, *It's not always about you, Joel.* He was jumping to conclusions because he felt guilty.

"My grandson is missing," Sally said. "My five-year-old grandson."

Or maybe it *was* about Joel this time.

How many little kids in a town this size went missing in a single night? Probably not more than one.

Joel had no idea what he should do now. Should he ask questions? That would be the normal thing to do, right? He had to act normal. Not guilty. Normal.

"Since when?" Joel blurted. Was that a good first question?

Apparently, it wasn't a bad one because Sally immediately answered it. "He wasn't in his bed when my daughter went to check on him, a little after midnight. She stays up late most nights. She's taking night classes, and that's when she studies, after Caleb goes to sleep. She always looks in on him before she goes to bed, and he wasn't there."

Sally reached into the pocket of her pink frilly apron and pulled out a handful of crumpled tissues. She blew her nose on one; her nose was as red as her eyes. "She didn't worry at first," she continued, "because Caleb is"—she sniffed, waved a hand, and tried a smile that looked more like a grimace—"a bit of a mischievous boy.

He likes to play pranks. He hates following rules. He's gone off on his own at least half a dozen times. He calls his adventures 'walkabouts.'" She sniffed again.

Joel was having trouble focusing on Sally's words. He had too much going on in his head to listen to her. First, there was his heartbeat, which was, for some reason, resounding off the inside of his skull. Second, there was the replay of the truck hitting the kid—it had a soundtrack in his mind: the squealing tires, the revving engine, the thud. Third, there was his inner dialogue:

You should say something.

Don't be an idiot. Say nothing. Just play dumb.

What if he's still alive?

Joel concentrated on turning down the volume on his brain's chatter so he could hear Sally. He didn't really *want* to hear her, but if he didn't act right when she talked, she could get suspicious.

"But she looked in all his usual favorite places in the house, in the neighborhood, even in the woods, and she called all his friends' parents," Sally went on. "When she still couldn't find him, well, that's when she called me. I told her to call the police. They've been looking for him since . . . what time is it?" She looked at her bare wrist.

Joel glanced at his watch.

"It's 5:03," he said.

"And you're here for . . . ?"

"Dad's donuts. But listen, I'll just go." Joel had to get out of here. Thinking about the kid in the ditch was one thing, but now thinking about *Caleb* lying in the ditch . . .

no, he couldn't do that. "Never mind the donuts," he said quickly. Then he added, "That's just awful about your grandson. I'm so sorry."

He turned and trotted out of the building before Sally could respond.

Three hours later, his nerves pulled so taut he figured he could probably pluck them like guitar strings, Joel followed his dad into Herb's Hardware in the middle of downtown. He had to concentrate to be sure his movements were casual and relaxed, not at all the way he felt.

Could he pull off this nonchalant act for the rest of the day?

When Joel had returned to his dad's truck, he'd had to explain why Sally hadn't made the donuts. And, of course, his dad had immediately gotten out of the truck and gone inside to talk to Sally. Not sure what he should do, Joel had remained in the truck, where he'd sat stiffly, chewing on his thumbnail.

He wasn't sure how long he'd sat there. Pretty long, he figured, because the sun was rising when his dad came back out.

Joel nearly jumped through the truck roof when his dad threw open the truck door and got back in. "The police chief is organizing a search," he said.

Joel blinked at his dad. "Huh?"

His dad shot him a look. "For Caleb. They're organizing a search."

Joel nodded and swallowed. He cleared his throat. "Has anyone seen . . . ?" he began. He was uneasy about asking any questions. What if someone *had* seen his truck near Glenwood Fields last night?

Joel's dad started his truck and put it in gear. "Montgomery and his officers are going door-to-door now. So far, no one's said they saw anything."

It was all Joel could do not to jump up and yell, "Yes!"

That was one worry he could set aside. All the time that he'd been telling himself he should go back and check on the kid, a nagging thought had been in the back of his mind: What if someone *had* seen what he'd done?

No one had.

So, if he said nothing, if he kept acting clueless, no one would know. He could go on with his life as if it never happened.

Yeah. As if he could forget it.

"We need to get back to the nursery," Joel's dad said. "I want you to get the deliveries loaded while I do a few things in the office. We'll open for a couple hours, but then we'll close up. We'll go help out with the search."

"Close?" Joel yelped. The only day he'd ever wanted to work, and they were going to close? Help with the search? Joel didn't want to be anywhere near the search.

"It's the right thing to do if Caleb isn't found right away. I've already talked to Montgomery on the phone. I told him we'd head over to the hardware store later this morning and get what we need to make some signs and maybe a command center for the search."

And here they were.

Herb's Hardware was in one of the town's oldest buildings. It had worn rough wood floors, high tin ceilings, and an old-fashioned cash register. The store smelled of wood, varnish, and dust. The shelves crammed with tools and home-improvement stuff went from floor to the super-high ceilings. Joel didn't think the top shelves had been cleaned in years.

Feeling like a little kid, Joel shadowed his dad as he strode through the store, gathering supplies for signs and a command center. He didn't complain about being here because ever since the kid he'd hit had been given a name, Joel had felt like he was sleepwalking. Or no. It was more like he wasn't in control of his own body. Part of him wanted to be a million miles away, not giving a crap about what was going on. And part of him wanted to go back to that ditch and see if the kid—if *Caleb*—was still alive. Because he couldn't bring himself to do either of these things, he was just numbly following his dad around.

"Get a bundle of those stakes," Joel's dad said, pointing.

Joel blinked and turned toward a shelf full of packaged wooden stakes as his dad went around the end of an aisle. Joel lifted a bundle and started to follow his dad again.

A clicking sound stopped him.

It was soft ticking, like plastic tapping on wood. And it was coming from behind him.

Joel whirled.

Nothing was there. He looked left and right and then down the aisle all the way to the picture window at the front of the store.

Something small and yellow caught his eye through the window. He sucked in his breath. Was that a—

He took a couple steps toward the window, squinting. It was.

A Kids at Play plastic figure was sitting outside the hardware store, right by the window. It was positioned so it looked like one of its black eyes was looking through the window, watching Joel.

Joel took a step back and thought hard. Had that been out front when he and his dad had gotten here?

He remembered seeing a row of rakes and wheel-barrows. Had there been a plastic Kids at Play figure, too? He shook his head. He didn't think so.

From behind him, the ticking sound started again. It sounded like small footsteps, footsteps made by plastic shoes . . . or plastic feet.

Joel held his breath and turned. Nothing.

Clutching the bundle of stakes, Joel hurried down the aisle to the back of the store. There, he turned left and headed into the hardware store's annex, an old add-on that contained work clothes—boots, gloves, overalls, and hats. He tried to tell himself he was imagining things, but then he heard the clicking again. The thing he was hearing was following him.

This time, Joel didn't even turn to look. He just took off again. He strode out of the annex and into the back of the store, ducking this way and that, around baskets of plumbing parts, lighting displays, and rows of power tools.

Everywhere he went, he heard that faint plasticky clicking following him.

He had to get out of here.

Joel made a turn to get back toward the front of the store. Head down, hugging the bundle of stakes like it was a teddy bear, he stepped forward . . . and ran right into his dad.

Joel yelped so loudly his voice echoed off the ceiling. He dropped the stakes.

"What are you doing?" his dad snapped.

"Umm." Joel ignored his dad and listened carefully. He didn't hear anything except his own uneven breathing.

"Pick that up and come on. I've got everything else by the counter," his dad said, then turned and walked away.

Joel picked up the stakes and meekly followed. He moved slowly, still listening for the clicking sound.

He heard nothing.

"You coming?" his dad asked.

Joel made his feet move. He followed his dad.

At the counter, Joel's dad paid for everything he'd stacked in their cart while Joel kept his back to the picture window. He didn't want to look at the yellowish figure. Instead, he listened for the clicking. Joel was still listening when his dad tugged on his sleeve. "What's wrong with you? I said we're ready to go."

Joel again followed his dad without speaking. When they stepped out through the front door, Joel made himself look over at the Kids at Play figure.

He noticed a price tag dangling from the figure's "hand." He screwed up his face in concentration. If the thing had a tag, it must have been here—for sale—when he and his dad had arrived. Why couldn't Joel remember seeing it?

Joel's day got better after he and his dad left the hardware store. He basically spent his afternoon on his own walkabout—nowhere near where Caleb was the night before. This was his part in the "search."

By the time late evening came, Caleb hadn't been found. Joel and his dad headed home and had dinner. Joel was still wound up tight, but his parents interpreted his behavior as worry for Caleb. In a way, it was. Or rather, it was worry for Joel *because* of Caleb.

Finally, Joel was able to get away with saying, "I'm beat. I'm going to go to bed so I can get up early and help out tomorrow, too."

As his parents said good night to him and his mother got in her, "And, Joel, you really must shower," he wondered how long it would be before Caleb's body—if it was in fact a "body" by now—would start to smell and attract animals. Caleb would be found then, surely. The ditch wasn't that far away from the houses.

Once again, as Joel went into his room, he heard the inner voice that told him it might not be too late. He might be able to save the boy.

You could be the hero, the voice said.

Yeah, Joel would be a hero . . . until the boy was well enough to describe who hit him. The boy had looked right at Joel in those few seconds while the truck skidded. The town was small enough that the boy could know who he was. Joel seemed to recall that Sally said her daughter went to the garden center all the time. Odds were that the kid had been there, too.

Nope. Joel couldn't risk "finding" Caleb.

Instead of doing something that could throw his life away, Joel took that shower his mom kept going on about. When he was done, he thought about messing around with his drum pads, but he really was wiped out.

Joel, in just his boxers—cool drummers didn't wear pj's—sat down on the edge of his bed. He turned on his bedside lamp. It immediately illuminated something that shouldn't have been there.

He gasped and jumped up. *What the hell?*

Joel gawked at the little plastic yellow figurine that stood next to his digital alarm clock, propped up against the base of his lamp. It was the figurine from the Fazcrunch box—that creepy little kid-shaped figure with its empty black eyes and its flag-at-attention warning, KIDS AT PLAY.

Joel had tossed that aside. When was that? Yesterday? Seemed like a month ago. Yeah, it was yesterday.

How did the figure get in his room?

Joel didn't have to think hard on that question. His mom probably found it and brought it up here to make a point. She hated when he left things lying around. When he was a little boy, she'd pick up after him. When he got into high school, though, she started just putting his stuff in a bin in the garage. He'd have to go out there and dig through the pile to find things like his softball glove, his Rollerblades, his sunglasses, or his earbuds.

Wait a minute. Yeah. Usually, she puts his stuff in the

garage. She never brings it up to his room. So why would she have brought this up?

Maybe his dad did it?

Whatever. It didn't matter how it got here.

Joel reached out and snatched up the figurine. As he stared at it, his muscles tensed. And suddenly, it felt like an ice cube was skittering down his spine. He shivered.

All the Kids at Play figures he'd seen today, that weird plastic clicking sound in the hardware store, and now this—it felt like he was being haunted by his conscience. *Do the right thing*, it was telling him. *Go back and save the kid. Save Caleb.*

Joel closed his hand over the figurine. He held it so tight that its edges cut into his palm.

The problem was that "the right thing" was right for Caleb, but it was wrong for Joel. If Joel went to the kid, whether Caleb was dead or alive, Joel could get in the kind of trouble that would mess him up for the rest of his life.

Really, the whole thing came down to the boundaries of life here that Joel so hated. If he was going to be free of them, he couldn't go check on Caleb. Doing that would not only keep Joel stuck in this town, it might literally put him in a jail cell. He wouldn't be able to survive that. Keeping quiet was a matter of self-preservation.

He shook his head. No way. He wasn't going to sacrifice his future for one stupid little kid who shouldn't have been running around in the dark in the middle of the night. *Who lets their kid do that?* Joel thought. He tried to tell himself it was only a matter of time before the kid got hurt. It just so happened to be that Joel was the unfortunate bystander who hit him. Really this was on the parents for not locking up the house or keeping an eye on their son.

Dropping the figurine onto his navy-and-beige Turkish carpet, Joel stomped on the ugly little dude until it broke into multiple pieces. When he noticed the KIDS AT PLAY flag was still unscathed, he reached down, picked it up, and snapped it into three pieces. He gave it one last look, ignoring the way the hair bristled at the back of his neck. Then he turned away from it.

He took a deep breath and let it out. For the first time all day, he felt relaxed. He'd made his decision, and he was okay with it.

Calmly getting into bed, Joel closed his eyes. Tonight, he wasn't tormented by doubt or by questions of right and wrong. He was perfectly satisfied that he'd done what he needed to do to look out for himself.

He went right to sleep.

Joel's eyes shot open. He blinked and looked around.

He'd been dreaming about the stupid little toy from the Fazcrunch box. But why had he awakened?

Joel rubbed his eyes and turned to check his bedside clock. It read 2:00 a.m. Exactly. That was weird. He couldn't remember the last time he'd woken up and the clock was right on the hour. It was . . .

Joel sat up.

Okay, that was *really* weird.

He hadn't planned on sitting up. He'd planned on closing his eyes and going back to sleep.

He didn't have to pee. He wasn't thirsty. He was still tired. Why would he sit up?

Joel threw back the covers and stood.

What the hell?

He didn't want to stand up. Why was he standing up?

Joel stood, ramrod straight and looked around the room as if his neck was on hydraulics. His head movement seemed stiff and jerky. What was wrong with him? His neck felt bizarre.

Come to think of it, his whole body felt off. It felt locked up and unyielding.

When Joel had been about eight, he'd gone out on a boat with Wes and his family, and he'd gotten badly sunburned. Not only had the burn hurt like crazy, it had made his skin so taut that he couldn't move properly. He felt a little like that . . . but worse.

It wasn't just his skin. His joints didn't feel right either. They felt like they did when he worked out too hard without warming up.

Joel's head turned to look at his chest of drawers. Now why was he looking over there?

Joel's leg lifted, and he took one step toward the chest. He tried not to. He had no reason to go over to his chest of drawers. He wanted nothing that was in it. Not right now. What he wanted was to go back to bed and sleep.

Instead, he took another step toward the chest.

He felt like his body wasn't his anymore.

He took another step. And another. And another.

Soon, he stood in front of his chest of drawers, and his arm lifted. His hand grasped the bronze knob on the drawer, and he pulled it open. He reached in and grabbed a fresh pair of jeans.

Every motion he made felt stiff, as if his joints had seized up and needed to be oiled so he could move properly. He was surprised he didn't creak or whir as he moved. His movements felt like those of the clunkiest of old-school androids.

No. His movements were even more basic than that. They didn't remind him of an old robot. They reminded him of a puppet, one of those wooden ones, with the strings attached to the joints. His motions weren't his own, like his body was being forced into motion. He could even hear his joints crack as they moved, as if they were protesting the directives being given to them.

As his hand closed the first drawer and opened the second to pull out a T-shirt, Joel concentrated hard on resisting his body's actions. He wanted to go back to bed! He imagined himself doing that, but imagining was all he could do.

Instead of going back to bed, he got dressed. Then he reached out to open his bedroom door.

The hall outside his room was dark and silent. The clock in his mother's office, a big grandfather clock she said was a family heirloom—like he cared—ticked loudly. From behind the closed door at the other end of the hall, his dad's snores attempted to drown out the clock's even rhythm.

Joel thought about calling out to his parents. Maybe

they could snap him out of whatever was going on with him. But he couldn't make a sound.

He walked, stiff-legged, down the hall to the top of the stairs. He then began a descent so awkward that several times he thought he was going to topple forward and fall, end over end, down the stairs. It wasn't that his body was moving wrong, it was that it was in such a state of resistance—his own body's will versus that of some outside force he didn't understand—that he was totally off balance.

Somehow, he reached the base of the steps. At this point, his body turned and pointed itself toward the kitchen. It made its way to the back door. There, using an arm that felt like a stone appendage, he brought up his hand to grab the knob.

Joel stepped off the back porch. He headed around the house toward the driveway.

He felt like he'd become a small version of himself and he was now trapped inside the large version. He was being taken for a ride by this big Joel creature who had an agenda little Joel knew nothing about.

Every time Joel swung a leg out, it felt like his leg belonged to someone else. Each time he planted his foot, he felt like his foot was in a cement shoe. But he kept walking; he strode, totally against his will, down the driveway to the road in front of his house.

The night was cooler than usual for this time of year. A breeze was coming down off the mountains, bringing with it the hint of a frost. Fragile spring green leaves fluttered on tree branches near the road. Fallen blossoms whispered as they skimmed over the pavement.

The night sky was similar to that of the previous night. Stars twinkled above, like all was right with the world, and an ever-so-slightly thicker wedge of moon sent pale rays of white light down to illuminate the cement in front of Joel. Even without the warm yellow glows reaching out from porch lights and lampposts in the yards along the street, he'd have been able to see just fine.

Not that it mattered what he was seeing.

Joel was pretty sure that even if he'd gone totally blind, he'd be moving along the street without a problem. He wasn't the one calling the shots. So why did he need to see anything?

His legs pivoting sluggishly at his hips, their rigid extensions lifting ahead of him like horizontal pistons, Joel headed down the street. After just a few steps like this, the creaking he'd thought he should hear when he was in his room actually began. Every time his leg raised out ahead of him, his joints rasped and groaned. It sounded like his joints were rusting. He'd heard lesser creaks from ancient oxidized gate hardware. The garden center had a gate with hinges like that. The sound they made was straight out of a horror movie: *cree—aaa—rrrr—eeek*. That's the way Joel's joints sounded as he walked.

But it wasn't the way his body *sounded* that concerned him. It was the way it felt.

Leaving aside the terrifying fact that he was no longer in control of his own movement, his body was starting to feel as unyielding as the granite up in the mountains that overlooked the town. Unfortunately, though, it didn't feel as strong as the granite. It felt, well, fragile. He felt like instead of being made of rock, or even wood, he was made of some kind of hard plastic.

And he felt like he was fragmenting, disconnecting from himself.

Joel didn't know how long he'd been walking because looking at his watch wasn't something his body wanted to do. However, given that he was now leaving his neighborhood, he guessed he'd been on this hijacked journey for at least ten minutes.

During whatever length of time he'd been out here, though, he'd noticed his body was starting to feel strained, as if it was reaching some sort of breaking point. He was starting to hear cracks interspersed with the creaks in his movement.

Were his bones fracturing?

He wasn't in horrible pain or anything. He just felt . . . *wrong*. He no longer felt like him, like a human. He was feeling more and more like a *thing*.

He was also feeling more and more panicked.

The panic rose as it became clear where his body was taking him.

When big Joel had gotten to the turn out of his neighborhood, he'd veered left on the cutover road that led to Glenwood Fields. Joel was heading back to where Caleb—or where Caleb's lifeless body—lay in a ditch.

Joel screamed in his mind. His mouth could no longer make sounds. It couldn't even open. It felt like it had been welded shut.

And it was just one of the systems in Joel's body that was shutting down.

In spite of the fact that Joel's movement had been labored, he couldn't help but notice he wasn't sweating, at all. Nor was he breathing heavily. He was scared, more scared than he could ever remember being. And yet, his heart wasn't racing. In fact, he couldn't sense any heartbeat. Usually, if he concentrated, he could feel his pulse. Not anymore. When he put his attention on his neck or his wrists, he felt nothing.

And now, as his panic began to morph into despair, he realized he couldn't generate tears either. He could feel that his face was an expressionless mask that in no way reflected how he felt on the inside. Anyone observing him would think he was perfectly calm.

Was anyone observing him?

Joel wanted to look around, to see if anyone was looking out their window at the freakish figure lumbering by. But did he really look freakish? Or did he just feel that way? He couldn't see himself, of course, but given how he felt, he didn't think that anything he was doing would look normal. He felt as if he was moving like a flash-frozen zombie. His surroundings seemed to shudder as he looked at them.

In spite of all the systems in Joel's body that were outside his control, his eyes were still his to use. He couldn't turn his head to look around, but he could see whatever was in front of him. And there, just a couple hundred yards away, were the entrance stones to Glenwood Fields.

Shaped vaguely like angel's wings, but dingy gray instead of white, the entrance signs were far grander than anything within the subdivision. Joel had always thought the houses in this area were pathetic—shallow-roofed structures shaped like Ls, with simple siding and plain small windows. Houses like these deserved a flimsy wood sign, not an elaborately carved set of huge stones.

As Joel got closer and closer to the stone markers, he noticed that they looked more like gravestones than entrance signs. That seemed oddly appropriate now, given that they marked the spot where Caleb likely lay dead.

Joel's mind offered up an image of a child's dead body, its face waxen, its eyeballs eaten by scavengers. As soon as this horrific visual flashed through his brain, his thoughts screamed, just as he would have if he'd seen something like that in real life.

Was he about to see something like that?

His feet, which he could no longer feel, were crunching through the gravel on the shoulder of the road by Glenwood Fields' entrance. He was no more than a couple yards from where the kid had been standing in the road when Joel had hit him. If Joel could have turned and taken two or three steps to his left, he would have been able to reach the edge of the ditch. He might have been able to look down the steep embankment to see whatever was lying in the narrow rocky bottom of the ditch. He would have been able to see for himself, finally, whether Caleb was dead.

But Joel couldn't turn, and he couldn't go anywhere he wasn't being compelled to go. He was not much different than a toy figurine at this point, subject to the whims of whoever or whatever wanted to position him.

And apparently, this was the spot.

Joel stopped moving. For several long seconds, Joel was still.

He could tell he was just off the pavement, right where he'd hit Caleb. He could even see the black snakelike track of his skid marks on the gray street.

Joel wondered if this was it. Would he be released now that he'd been brought to this point? Had the whole purpose of this body snatching been to get him where he'd refused to go?

Joel didn't get much of a chance to ponder this question before the answer revealed itself.

No, this was not it. His ordeal was not over.

In fact, it was about to get much, much worse.

Joel felt an ache begin in his mouth, at the roots of his teeth. It was a dull pain, but it was noticeable. What did it mean? What was happening in his mouth?

Jake was now so terrified that he felt a scream climb up his throat and into his mouth. But it didn't come out. It couldn't. Joel wasn't able to control his vocal cords.

Joel did, however, open his mouth for the first time since he left his house. Apparently, it wasn't welded shut because he could sense his lips hinging apart. He even heard the opening. A little smack and suctioning sound preceded the sensation of air moving against his gums and his tongue. That sensation was barely noticeable because of how much the pain in his teeth commanded his attention, but he knew it meant his mouth was open.

Suddenly the pain in his teeth stopped, and he felt something different. He heard something different, too.

The sound he heard was a quiet clicking, a faint intermittent tapping like the sound of pebbles dribbling to the ground. It felt like pebbles falling too . . . in his mouth. Small hard bits were dropping onto his tongue and tumbling past his lips.

No. Not small, hard bits.

Teeth.

One of the bits rolled across his lower lip in a way that allowed him to feel the smooth surface on one side and the rough surface on an adjacent side. He also felt the triangular shape of the end of the bit. It *was* a tooth. The sound he was hearing was his teeth landing among the small, jagged rocks that made up the gravel beside the road.

While Joel tried to make sense of this inexplicable event, he felt one of the bits fall back, down his tongue. It lodged in his throat, and he felt like he was gagging. He wanted to—needed to—cough up the tooth and spit it out, but he couldn't control his neck muscles any more than he could control any other part of his body. All he could do was imagine himself choking to death while the tooth stuck to his throat.

Crazed with disbelief, Joel's inner voice shrieked and shrieked and shrieked. But his inner voice had no volume. No one could hear him because he made no sound.

His sight, his hearing, and his ability to feel pain were the only things Joel had left. He was pathetically grateful for these small gifts . . . until his eyes showed him what was happening next.

A tuft of black hair fluttered out in front of Joel's vision. It got caught on a current in the night's breeze, and it wafted away. Another tuft followed the first. Then a third, then a fourth. Then chunks of hair started dropping in front of his eyes. He felt more hunks slip down the back of his neck. Joel's hair was falling out.

His silent shrieks turned into wails.

Joel's consciousness, trapped within his traitorous body, could do nothing with the outrage and despair that strangled him from within. Every reaction he was having to the unspeakable things happening to him was being consumed by the black void of whatever controlled him.

Make it stop, Joel thought. He didn't know who he was addressing. It was a universal appeal, a weak command from a peon in a universe that didn't care.

Joel didn't want to see anymore. He couldn't take watching another piece of who he thought he was falling away.

Perhaps because he literally couldn't withstand the trauma of seeing anything else, his "wish" was granted.

Joel's eyes dropped out of his head. He actually felt them disconnect and roll down his cheeks.

As soon as his eyes left his body, he went blind. As horrifying as this was, at least Joel didn't have to watch his eyeballs drop to the gravel beneath his feet. He didn't have to see a sharp point of basalt puncture one of the brown irises.

He did hear it, though. His ears ever-so-helpfully delivered to him the sickening *splat* of his eyes reaching the ground.

His ears were also still doing their duty when Joel's fingers fell away from his hands. He heard his fingers clatter onto the ground like sticks hitting rocks.

Before he could even begin to process this inconceivable mutilation, his hands disconnected from his arms. It felt like wires wrapped around the tendons and tore his hands from his wrists.

He heard what was left of his hands land beneath him. The sound was a crunchy *thwack*, similar to what he once heard when he'd accidentally dropped his empty orange juice glass in his Fazcrunch cereal.

For a second, Joel was nauseated by the sound. But only for a second. He didn't have time to linger for long over the sound of his hands hitting the ground because his awareness was immediately yanked to a new form of suffering.

Now he could feel something pushing its way out through his empty eye sockets. It felt like some pulsing form was being pumped through the openings, something like a balloon or a ball being inflated. He could feel the pressure around the space where his eyes used to be. The pressure built and built until he could sense whatever had been inflated was protruding out over his cheekbones.

Once again, he didn't have long to think about this new abomination because the following one started immediately. The next thing to terrorize him was his skin.

He felt his skin beginning to snap apart and slip from his body. The sensation was similar to what he'd felt when sunburned skin started to peel, but it was much stronger than that . . . because it wasn't just the top layer of skin that was unraveling from him; it was *every* layer. His skin was flaying away from his muscles and his tendons. As his skin parted from what was beneath it, he felt the breeze sting his exposed tissues.

It felt like some unseen hand was pulling his skin from his body, paring wet sections from him as if he was a fish being filleted. He could hear the soggy strips slap the ground. He knew long ribbons of his skin were piling up beneath him because every sinew of his body felt exposed.

Joel knew . . .

Nothing.

Finally, after being subjected to more heinous misery than any human could have been expected to survive, his consciousness succumbed to whatever force was orchestrating his transformation. The person that was Joel ceased to exist.

The partial moon dripped the palest of white glows above the tall mountain peaks east of town when Chief Montgomery's SUV rounded the corner and stopped just inside the stone-marked Glenwood Fields entrance. His radio squawked as soon as he turned off his engine. He picked up his mic, keyed it on, and listened.

"Chief," his dispatcher said, "I just got confirmation from that Glenwood resident that the strange man he saw was headed toward the entrance."

"That's where I am," the chief responded. "I'll check it out." He put the mic back into its holder and got out of his SUV.

The angle at which the moon brushed the mountain range told the chief it was about 3:00 a.m. or so. Night still wrapped its blanket around his town.

A surprisingly small man whose personality and authority didn't match his short stature, the chief grabbed his hat and pulled it over thinning brown hair. He hefted his flashlight and got out of his vehicle.

Chief Montgomery held his flashlight stiffly as he aimed it around the subdivision entrance. He'd been tense all day, ever since Jenna Bell had called him in the early morning hours the day before. The long hours that Caleb had been missing had taken a toll on Montgomery and his officers. He felt like he'd aged at least five years since that call. Several times during the day, he'd told Jenna everything would be all right. But he wasn't sure he believed it.

The chief turned in a slow circle, scanning the areas illuminated by the glow of his flashlight. He didn't see anything at first. But then he did.

He froze, concentrating on the strange shape hunched in the shadows just beyond the range of his flashlight. He stepped forward so his light would land directly on the form.

Montgomery gulped and took a step back. He immediately felt silly. His response had been ridiculous. What he was looking at was nothing to be upset about.

The chief's flashlight beam lit up a large, misshapen plastic boy positioned right at the edge of the road. The plastic figure had a mostly featureless face—no nose, no cheeks, no chin. All the face had was two bulging black eyes and an open, darkness-filled mouth.

Montgomery had seen a few figures like this around town. It was part of some Freddy Fazbear public safety initiative to deter reckless drivers in areas where kids were running around. Most of the figures he'd seen were much smaller than this one, and this one was oddly contorted, as if some of the plastic had been deformed in the molding process.

For some reason, the shape disturbed the chief. He was spooked, but he couldn't possibly have explained why if anyone had asked him.

He shook his head. He was just overtired; that was all. Too much stress. The chief started to move on and search beyond the bizarre figure, but then his light landed on something piled up on the ground. He tilted his flashlight downward and frowned in confusion. What was that? Mulch? What was mulch doing out on the road?

Leaning closer, he shined his light over what looked like glistening pinkish-brown ribbons tangled together. Not ribbon, obviously. The mass of material appeared to be something organic, and for some reason, it gave him the heebie-jeebies. He shook off the shiver that ran through him.

The ribbon-like lengths looked a little like freshly stripped bark. He glanced to the side of the road, at the trees clustered near the subdivision's entrance, looking to see if a tree had been ravaged by a vandal or maybe an animal. All of the trees looked okay, but . . .

From the left of the trees he was focused on, Montgomery heard a whimper. He froze and listened.

Was that really a whimper, or the cry of some injured animal?

He tilted his head and concentrated.

And there it was again.

That wasn't an animal! It sounded like a child.

The chief immediately shifted his light toward the ditch at the side of the road. That was where the sound was coming from.

He hurried over to the edge of the road and aimed his light into the ditch. He couldn't see anything.

"Hello?" he called out. "Caleb?"

The whimper turned into a cry.

Montgomery turned and ran toward his SUV. Reaching for his mic, he keyed it on. "Rankin, get the EMTs out here to the Glenwood Fields entrance. I think I've found the kid!"

He didn't wait for a response. He spun around and ran past the weird Kids at Play figure. When he got to the edge of the ditch, he slid down its side. "I'm coming, Caleb. Hang on!"

The weak cry that answered him made his heart leap with hope. He scrabbled toward the sound, and when he saw the small boy wedged behind a pile of rock, he dropped to his knees.

"I'm here, Caleb. It's okay. You're going to be okay."

As Chief Montgomery took off his jacket and laid it over the boy's narrow shoulders, he couldn't help but grin in triumph. He'd found the kid! Everything was going to be all right.

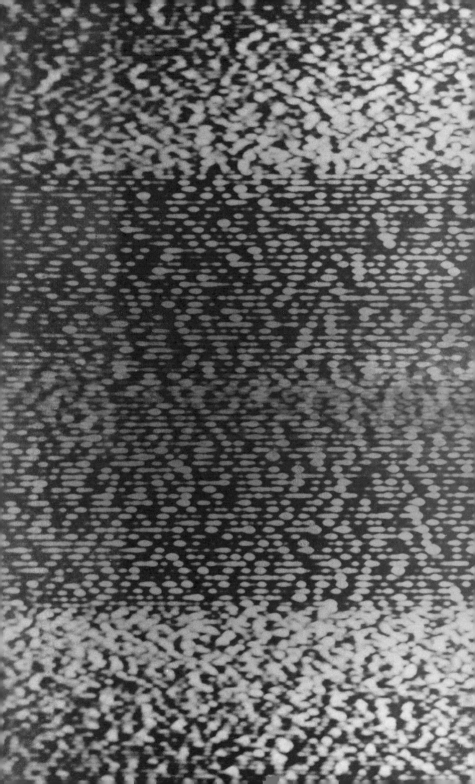

"**Y**ou are so gross!" Aimee turned her head away from her friend. "I can't even look at you."

Mary Jo's *rat-a-tat-tat* laugh spewed across the table at Aimee, along with some of her partially chewed pizza. She'd been showing off how she could flip a mouthful of pizza on her tongue, "Just like they flip the whole pizzas in the oven."

Who did that? It was disgusting.

Without looking at it, Aimee flicked away whatever had just landed on her forearm. She felt a wadded-up napkin hit her on the cheek. She sighed and turned back toward Mary Jo, careful to keep her eyes squinted in case Mary Jo was doing something else that was grody.

"Why do you do stuff like that?" Aimee asked.

Mary Jo laughed again. "Because I can."

Aimee shook her head. How was it she'd been friends with this freak of nature for eight years?

Instead of being at home, curled up in her cozy room on her frilly pink window seat, reading the book her dad had bought for her on his latest business trip, Aimee sat across from Mary Jo in one of the red booths at Freddy Fazbear's Pizza, a half-eaten slice on the table between them. On the stage to their right, the pizzeria's animatronic performers—Freddy, the brown bear in the top hat; Bonnie, the blue rabbit with the red bow tie; and Chica, the yellow chick with the bib and the mouthy pink cupcake with googly eyes—were performing a toe-tapping rock song. The music was loud, but it still didn't drown out all the other noise in the restaurant. The place was filled with animated conversation, laughter, happy squeals, utensils clinking against plates, and the pings and beeps and warbles from the games in the arcade just off the dining room.

Although Aimee liked the pizza, she didn't enjoy the raucous chaos at Freddy's. She was a quiet girl, more content by herself than in crowds.

Mary Jo, on the other hand, *loved* the craziness at Freddy's. She especially loved the music. At the moment, she was bobbing in her seat, right on beat with the music.

rhythm—bouncing on the offbeat. Mary Jo's hair, like Mary Jo herself, had always had a mind of its own, even when she was three. When Aimee had worn her blonde hair in pigtails, a braid, or a ponytail in preschool—like nearly all the other three-year-old girls, Mary Jo never wanted to restrain her hair. She refused to let her mother control it with hair ties or braids or clips. She wanted it to fly out from her head like a lion's mane, wild and free, the way Mary Jo liked to be. And even back then, Mary Jo usually got what she wanted.

Mary Jo and Aimee were exact opposites. That's why they had been friends for so long, according to Aimee's mom. They balanced each other out.

Like right now. Aimee was frowning, her face screwed up in protest of the noise and her weirdo friend's antics. Mary Jo was smiling widely, flashing her big mouthful of equally big teeth, now stained with sauce from the pizza. Yuck. She had sauce on her round cheeks, too. Aimee didn't bother to tell Mary Jo about the sauce. Mary Jo wouldn't care; she might even go so far as to put sauce on the other side, too, and call it war paint. Whatever was normal was often the opposite of what Mary Jo wanted to do.

Mary Jo took another big bite of pizza, chewing with her mouth open. Aimee made a face and pushed away the remains of the piece in front of her. She'd lost her appetite, which was never as big as Mary Jo's anyway.

"Are you done?" Mary Jo asked.

Aimee nodded. She didn't bother to explain why.

"You need to eat more. You're bony," Mary Jo said.

"So what? You're pudgy. You're always saying not everyone should be alike."

Mary Jo swallowed her pizza—thank goodness—and picked up her soda to take a long suck through the straw. The clackety-suctioning sound that indicated the bottom of the glass prompted her to pull back and scowl at the ice cubes that remained.

"You're right, I'm wrong," Mary Jo said. "Okay, so if you're done, do you want to play in the Hiding Maze?"

Aimee shrugged and nodded. She still would rather be home reading, but she'd predicted Mary Jo would want to play in the Hiding Maze, so she'd brought a new book with her. It was tucked into the cute fanny pack her mom had bought her, along with strawberry-flavored lip gloss, her hair brush, and some money.

The Hiding Maze, short for Freddy's Hiding Maze, was a fancy hide-and-seek game played in a network of tunnels that ran between the walls enclosing Freddy's main areas—dining, arcade, kitchen, restrooms, storage, stage, etc.—and the exterior walls of the restaurant. It was pretty cool, actually. The hiding places were little cubby-holes with doors; the doors had tiny windows you could peer out of when you were hiding—probably so kids didn't feel trapped. The windows were made of that special glass that looked like a window on one side and a mirror on the other. If you were a seeker, you could only see the mirrors on the cubbyholes as you walked down the tunnel, while hiders could look out without being spotted. Even though the game and its cubbyholes some-times made Aimee a little nervous, the hidey-holes were cool for a different reason: They appealed to Aimee's natural desire to be by herself. Only two people played the Hiding Maze at a time, so when you were in the game tunnels, you were far from all the craziness in the rest of the restaurant.

When she and Mary Jo played, Aimee always preferred being the hider, and Mary Jo loved being the seeker. Mary Jo was never happy sitting still. She liked to be *doing* something, and she loved a challenge. Aimee assumed this was why school was so hard for her friend. Mary Jo was bored out of her mind in the classroom. She was constantly getting caught doodling in the margins of her notebook instead of taking notes while the teacher was talking. *But really, it's more than doodling*, Aimee thought. Mary Jo didn't draw actual things, like *recognizable* things—she made patterns and shapes was all—but they were supercool patterns and shapes. Aimee had seen stuff like it in an art museum her mom took her to once. She had tried to tell Mary Jo she had talent, but Mary Jo shrugged it off. "Nah. I'm not talented. I'm just a pain in the butt with a good friend." Aimee had hugged Mary Jo then, feeling a big wave of affection for the girl who often made her want to scream.

The Hiding Maze was a great way for both girls to do the things they liked, together—sort of. It worked because Aimee had figured out a way to cheat . . . in reverse. Because of the way she played, Aimee got some quiet time, and Mary Jo got a challenge.

"So, are you going to sit there, or are you coming?" Mary Jo asked.

Aimee blinked and looked up at Mary Jo, who was dancing around at the end of their booth, shrugging into her backpack and doing odd gyrations to the music at the same time.

"Oh, sorry. I was thinking."

"You do too much of that." Mary Jo laughed loudly and punched Aimee in the arm.

Aimee squealed and rubbed her arm. That was another thing Mary Jo was good at: throwing an unintentionally hard punch.

When Aimee and Mary Jo had met at age three, they'd both been small for their age. Other than that, they hadn't had much in common . . . and they still didn't. Aimee was light haired and pale skinned and had small features with bright-blue eyes. Mary Jo had that brown frizzy hair and large mouth, along with caramel-colored skin, big brown eyes, and a wide nose. As they grew up, their size similarity changed, too. Aimee remained small, but Mary Jo shot both up and out. She was six inches taller than Aimee now, and as Aimee had reminded her, she was pudgy. She was also a lot stronger than Aimee, both physically and in all other ways, actually.

Sometimes, Aimee thought about not being friends with Mary Jo anymore. They had so little in common. But Aimee would never have the heart to dump Mary Jo as a friend. Mary Jo had gone through enough dumping.

Mary Jo's parents were really young when they got married and had their daughter. *Too young*, according to Aimee's mom. Mary Jo's dad left his wife and daughter when Mary Jo was just a baby. Mary Jo's mom had tried to take care of her daughter after that, but she gave up when Mary Jo was five. One day, she just left, and Mary Jo ended up in foster care. That's where she still was, now on her fifth foster family.

Aimee had asked her parents to take in Mary Jo on more than one occasion, but her mom said they didn't have the "resources" to "handle" Aimee's friend. She didn't mean money. Even though she was just a kid, Aimee knew her family had plenty of money. Aimee's mom meant time and patience. Aimee's parents both worked important jobs. Her dad was a "high-level manager," which meant her dad told other people what to do. Her mom was a "marketing consultant," which meant her mom advised other people on how to sell their brands and stuff. Aimee's parents had a lot to do and a lot of people depending on them.

If Aimee had to be honest, though, she was sometimes glad Mary Jo hadn't come to live with them. She loved Mary Jo, but Mary Jo could be very annoying . . . displays of partially chewed food being just one good example. Mary Jo could be really yucky when she wanted to be. Sometimes Aimee wondered if that was a by-product of her tough upbringing. It was like she *wanted* people to look at her, whether for a good or bad reason.

"Well?" Mary Jo asked. "Do I need to punch you again?"

Aimee blinked. "What? Oh, no. Don't punch me again! I swear I'll stop thinking. Let's go play in the Hiding Maze."

Mary Jo grinned and took Aimee's arm. Skipping,

she began pulling Aimee toward the arcade. All Aimee could do was follow, scowling at Mary Jo's back as Mary Jo yanked her between the tables and around other kids. Mary Jo's overstuffed backpack made it look like she had a hump on her shoulders.

According to Aimee's mom, Mary Jo *would* have a real hump if she kept carrying her backpack around everywhere. "The way she hunches her shoulders to carry all that weight," Aimee's mom often said, "it's not good for her."

Aimee had told Mary Jo about what her mom had said, but Mary Jo laughed it off. "So what if I end up with a hunchback, like some old witch?" She curled forward, squinted her eyes, put her hands into claw shapes, and cackled like a wicked witch. "That'd be fine. No one would mess with me if I looked like that."

"You're weird," Aimee had said.

"You're not," Mary Jo had responded. "I think not being weird is worse."

Aimee knew why Mary Jo carried her bulging pack with her wherever she went. One day, when she was throwing a fit over something one of the other foster kids had done, Mary Jo had shown Aimee everything in her pack: her favorite clothes, a picture of her mom, her hug-worn teddy bear, her pillow, pens, crayons, a couple of books, pj's, slippers, a big detangling hairbrush Aimee didn't think Mary Jo *ever* used, her toothbrush, her zipper purse filled with a few dollars and some coins, a few battered candy bars, a bag of peanuts, and her diary. "I can leave whenever I want," Mary Jo had said. "See? I have what I need."

"Where would you go?" Aimee had asked.

Mary Jo had shrugged. "I don't have to plan every-thing, do I? I'll just go."

Gazing at Mary Jo's backpack now, Aimee wondered whether it still had all the same stuff in it. It had been a year, at least, since Mary Jo had showed Aimee what was in the pack. Had she added anything? Had she taken any-thing away?

Aimee let her friend drag her all the way through Freddy's packed dining room full of big round tables sur-rounded by laughing families. At least they hadn't been sitting out here. That was one thing she and Mary Jo agreed on—they preferred the booths to the tables. The booths were separated from one another by low dividers painted with cartoonlike images of the animatronic characters. It made each booth seem like its own little room.

Mary Jo kept pulling Aimee, and Aimee went along until they were just inside the edge of the arcade. There, however, Aimee faltered. Then she stopped. Something—no, someone—a man—had caught her eye.

"Aimee, what are you doing?" Mary Jo asked. Actually, she shouted. She had to shout to be heard over all the screams and dings and sirens in the game area.

But when she shouted, the man Aimee had spotted turned to look at the girls. Aimee flushed and stood on her tiptoes so she could whisper in Mary Jo's ear. "There's something creepy about that man over there."

Mary Jo immediately looked around. "What man?" she asked in yet another shout.

Aimee winced when the man shifted his attention fully to Mary Jo.

"Shh," Aimee hissed. "Come on." She tugged on Mary Jo's arm.

But Mary Jo pulled away. She took two steps toward the man, put her hands on her hips, and yelled out, "It's not polite to stare, creep!"

"*Mary Jo!*" Aimee whispered intensely.

Aimee felt the hair on the back of her neck stand up from her skin as she watched the man, a tall and skinny guy with long, greasy hair, give Mary Jo the kind of grin Aimee's mother would have called "impertinent." The guy's dark, almost-black eyes were narrowed with unnerving intensity. He had yellowed and crooked teeth, and his face reminded Aimee of one of those scary wrinkled Halloween masks. All the guy needed was some blood dripping from his mouth, and he could have been the bad guy in a horror movie. Wearing stained, baggy clothes, he looked like a street person. What was he doing in Freddy's?

"Come on," Aimee urged Mary Jo.

Mary Jo wouldn't budge. She jutted out her lower jaw in an act of defiance and squinted at the man. "You want a piece of me, creep?"

Aimee rolled her eyes and groaned. Mary Jo watched too many cop shows.

Aimee tried tugging on Mary Jo again.

Mary Jo suddenly laughed, and Aimee dropped her arm.

"What . . . ?" Aimee began.

Then she saw that the man was gone.

Mary Jo spun in a circle and did a little boxing motion. "Nobody messes with me or my friend!" she yelled out.

The other kids in the arcade looked over at her for a few seconds. Some of the kids gave her dirty looks. Then all the kids returned to their games.

Mary Jo took Aimee's arm. "Stick with me. I'll protect you from the creepazoids."

Aimee smiled but then shivered. She glanced toward where the man had been standing. He *was* gone . . . Aimee hoped.

"How about we do something different today?" Mary Jo asked as they approached the beige grate that covered the rainbow-colored entrance to the Hiding Maze game.

Aimee loved that the entrance to the Hiding Maze game didn't look like the entrance to a game. It just looked like a heater vent cover or something surrounded by an arched rainbow. She knew that most parents didn't even know the game existed. The rainbow looked like a wall decoration, not the start of a game. Aimee and Mary Jo had only learned about the game a year or so before. By then, they'd been coming to Freddy's for several years.

One day, a little blond kid named Alby, who Aimee and Mary Jo only knew from Freddy's, came over and said, "You've been coming here enough. We think you're ready."

"Ready for what?" Mary Jo had asked.

Alby had just grinned and told them to follow him. He'd led them back here to this grate surrounded by the rainbow. Mary Jo had threatened to beat him up if he was going to do something mean to them. He'd just rolled his eyes and opened the grate. Then he'd pointed at a digital game display, which was on the left wall of a small, low, box-shaped chamber just beyond the grate.

With walls of knotted pine and a red floor covered with a multicolored rag rug, the tiny space looked like an elf's living room. It was just big enough for a couple of kids, crawling or sitting down. The room contained the grate-covered entrance on one wall; the game console and framed pictures of Freddy, Bonnie, and Chica on another wall; and a red vinyl mini-sofa big enough for two kids to sit on against a third wall. The wall behind the sofa was painted with a mural of thick evergreen trees dripping with moss. The scene reflected the look of the game itself. On the fourth wall, opposite the grate, a round opening revealed a long, dim tunnel.

Above the display in the elfin living room, where the players' names were put in, the name of the game was printed in black block letters: FREDDY'S HIDING MAZE HIDE-AND-SEEK GAME. Next to the game's name, an image of Freddy had a speech bubble. The rules of the game were printed inside that bubble.

Aimee thought it was cool that they were now part of something that seemed like a secret club. So did Mary Jo. Mary Jo liked it even more than Aimee did, probably because she didn't get to be part of anything else, secret or not.

"What do you want to do differently?" Aimee asked now as she dropped to her knees, pulled open the grate, and crawled through the opening behind it. She gave a half second's thought to the cute raspberry-colored capri pants she was wearing—they'd be filthy when they were done with the game. She shouldn't have worn them today, but she couldn't help herself.

Aimee could hear the scuffles and grunts of Mary Jo following her. Mary Jo didn't care about her clothes. She was usually dressed as she was today—in stained jeans and a too-tight T-shirt.

Once she was inside the little game entrance room, Aimee looked at the console. The display would have players' names on it if a game was in progress. It would be blank if no one was in the game.

Two names were on the display, and Freddy's voice announced, "Welcome to Freddy's Hiding Maze Hide-and-Seek Game. Please wait. A game is currently in progress."

Aimee crawled over and sat on one end of the red sofa. Mary Jo shifted and planted her butt on the other end. She had to bend forward because of her backpack.

Turning to look at Aimee, Mary Jo said, "I want to be Player Two first today."

"What?" Aimee rotated to stare at her friend. "I'm always Player Two first. I hide first. You seek first. That's how we always do it."

"I know. Boring, right? We need to mix it up," Mary Jo said.

Aimee opened her mouth to object, mostly just because she didn't like the way Mary Jo bossed her around. But really? Did it matter that much? She shrugged. "Whatever."

Mary Jo crossed her arms and closed her eyes, looking pleased with herself.

Aimee cocked her head and studied Mary Jo. She looked the same way Aimee's cat looked when she sat in a sunbeam with her eyes closed. Aimee always thought her cat looked stuck-up when she did that. Mary Jo did, too.

Aimee opened her mouth to ask Mary Jo why she always had to get her way, but then Freddy's voice announced, "Ready for new Player One and Player Two. Please input player names."

When Aimee was very little, she'd thought Freddy was actually inside the games that had his voice. Now that she understood they were programmed prerecorded voices, she always laughed at herself when she heard the games' audio.

Mary Jo opened her eyes and pointed toward the console. "Go on. You're Player One."

Aimee glared at Mary Jo. "Fine, Miss Bossy Pants."

Mary Jo gave Aimee a huge grin.

Aimee snorted. "You're incorrigible." She'd just learned that word the week before. It fit Mary Jo perfectly. She really couldn't be corrected or improved. She was always going to be just as she was now.

Mary Jo grinned even wider and blew a kiss to Aimee. "I love you, too." She pointed at the game console again. "Go on. If you can find me in three minutes, I promise we'll spend the rest of the day doing what you want to do . . . after we play both rounds."

"I want to read my new book."

Mary Jo stuck her finger in her mouth and made a gagging sound. Then she laughed at the look Aimee gave her. "Fine. We'll go to your house and sit in your room.

You can read, and I guess I'll draw . . . *if* you find me in three minutes."

"And if I don't?"

"We'll keep doing what I want to do."

Aimee sighed. "Fine." She crawled over, knelt in front of the game console, and typed in her name as Player One and Mary Jo's name as Player Two. As soon as she finished with Mary Jo's name, the Freddy voice said, "Player Two, please find your hiding place."

Aimee turned, stuck her tongue out at her bright-eyed, wild-haired friend, then returned to the little sofa. That was where the seeker was supposed to wait while the hider went to hide.

Mary Jo flashed Aimee with a huge smile and waved before disappearing into the main tunnel. "Good luck finding me," she called out.

Aimee didn't bother to answer. She just crossed her arms and sighed. She was tempted to get out her book, but if Mary Jo chose a spot quickly, Aimee would waste precious minutes putting her book away. So, she just sat and waited. She counted to see how long Mary Jo took to hide.

Aimee had just whispered, "107," when Freddy's voice announced, "Player Two has chosen a hiding spot! Player One, find Player Two! Go!" Aimee scooted off the sofa and started crawling through the main tunnel as fast as she could go.

"Fast" wasn't really that fast in the Hiding Maze. All the tunnels in the Hiding Maze game were sloped. Some went up and some went down; none were perfectly level. Most of the tunnels curved this way and that. They were constricting and confining, with ceilings that often felt like they were pressing downward, trying to bury you alive. Only the main tunnel was straight, but it went uphill. Aimee couldn't go as fast as she wanted to.

The Hiding Maze was designed so that only half the hiding cubbyholes were open at the start of the game. When Player Two found a hiding place, the door of that cubbyhole and all the other open cubbyhole doors were closed. The doors that had been closed then opened. So, Aimee didn't have to search the entire maze, but just searching the closed doors would take long enough.

Every tunnel in the maze was lined with the rough spongy material, colored to look like the bark of evergreen trees, like the ones in the mural. They weren't real trees, of course, but they felt like it. They smelled like it, too. The whole Hiding Maze had a musty, earthy smell that always made Aimee feel like she was crawling around in dirt burrows. The floor of the tunnels even looked like dirt: brown and uneven and kind of squishy like wet mud. Aimee didn't know what the tunnels were made of—not mud, obviously, because she never got muddy.

Interspersed between the trees, big gray fake boulders created nooks and crannies for the hiding cubbyholes. Each hiding cubbyhole was covered with an arched wood door that looked like the entrance to an elf's or fairy's home. The little viewing one-way windows were round insets in the upper part of the doors.

From the tops of the tunnels, fake tree branches tickled the top of Aimee's head as she passed under them. They were loaded with fine moss that looked like silky green hair, which made them hang low and heavy. Occasionally, one strand would flutter over her face and make her feel like she was going to sneeze.

Aimee thought the whole Hiding Maze was kind of spooky, especially because the trees weren't the only thing lining the walls. Here and there, little plump gray wormlike things wiggled as you went by. They had googly eyes that rolled around. Aimee tried not to look at them. In a few places, just mechanical eyes peered out between the tree trunks. Those eyes rolled around, too, and they bothered Aimee more than the worms because she imagined the eyes belonged to awful creatures lurking behind the trees.

The tunnels weren't so dark that they were *terrifying* to be in, though. Strings of rope lights that looked like tree roots lined the bottom and top edges of the tunnels and surrounded each cubbyhole. But it was still kind of an eerie place. The game had its own soundtrack, which played on a loop from a dinged-up old cassette tape that was warping in places. The track was mostly rain forest sounds, some of them soothing, like the constant patter of a steady downpour, spattering the trees and forest floor. But every now and then, other sounds would cut in: creepy screeches that could have been monkeys . . . or maybe jaguars. When you were hiding, you felt kind of safe, sheltered from the noise, secure in your chosen cubbyhole. When you were seeking, the soundtrack put you on edge; the growls and shrieks never failed to give Aimee goose bumps.

Everything about the Hiding Maze felt old to Aimee.

She wasn't sure how long Freddy's had been here, but the Hiding Maze seemed ancient. In addition to the game's worn soundtrack, a lot of the tree bark and moss were breaking off, and the cubbyhole doors were scratched and warped. It felt to Aimee like the Hiding Maze had been a big deal at one point, but now it was mostly forgotten, so it wasn't being maintained.

Even though the floors of the Hiding Maze tunnels weren't made of real dirt, they were always dirty—covered with scuff marks and food stains and littered with debris left behind by other seekers. She was pretty sure the Freddy's employees never cleaned back here. Aimee saw some confetti sprinkled along the edges of the passageway she crawled through and a deflated balloon lying outside one of the cubbyhole doors—those had been here for months now. Some kid had lost a striped sock with a hole in the toe just a few feet into the main tunnel.

Aimee had lost something in the maze a few months before. Mary Jo had made her a red-beaded friendship bracelet, and Aimee had noticed it was missing from her wrist after one of their games in the Hiding Maze. She'd thought Mary Jo would be upset about the loss, but Mary Jo had just shrugged and said, "It's probably in one of the cubbyholes. We'll find it one of these days." They hadn't found it yet.

You weren't supposed to bring food inside the Hiding Maze, but most kids didn't follow that rule. Right now, for example, the tunnel smelled strongly of chocolate, and Aimee had to crawl around a few fresh, glistening brown stains on the side of one of the boulders—some kid must have brought chocolate cake in here. He (she guessed it was a boy) had even left a broken red plastic fork behind.

As she neared the end of the main tunnel's first leg, she spied the other game console, which displayed her name as Player One and Mary Jo's name as Player Two, and a running timer showing how long it had been since the game had started.

Staring at the bright timer against the relative dark of the tunnel, Aimee's head started to hurt. She noticed she was grinding her teeth, something she did when she was upset. That always made her head hurt. She concentrated on relaxing her teeth, but the ache remained. She was tired of always going along with whatever Mary Jo wanted.

Aimee reached a closed cubbyhole door and lifted its little round metal handle. It clicked when she lifted it. Peering into the empty cubbyhole (of course she wouldn't find Mary Jo that easily), Aimee regretted their three-minute bargain. There was no way she was going to win that fast.

Aimee wasn't sure how long it would take to crawl up and down every meandering tunnel in the Hiding Maze. She'd never done that. But she knew it would take way longer than three minutes.

The Hiding Maze rules allowed Player One to search for Player Two for as long as it took to find Player Two's hiding spot. However, the game also allowed Player One to give up if he or she got tired of looking. Win or lose, Player One and Player Two switched places after the first round of play. The truth was that Aimee had never even *tried* to find Mary Jo in the Hiding Maze before. She liked to be the hider first because she could get her book out and read while she hid. Mary Jo never gave up, and sometimes it took her a long time to find Aimee. Aimee read until Mary Jo found her. Once they switched places for Round Two and Mary Jo was hidden, Aimee would usually just sit in the tunnel and read some more. Mary Jo thought Aimee was searching for her, but Aimee was actually just hanging out. After a little while, she'd press the "Give Up" button on the game console, and all the cubbyhole doors would open. At that point, Aimee would put her book away and meet Mary Jo outside the game, congratulating her on another win.

Going first meant Aimee couldn't pull off this trick as easily. And taking the bet meant she couldn't do it at all.

Now, frustrated and tired with her growing headache, Aimee was tempted to just sit in the tunnel and read for her remaining minutes before pressing "Give Up," but she really didn't want to hang around Freddy's all afternoon. So, for once, she tried to find her friend.

Wriggling through the first few twists and turns off the main corridor, Aimee threw open cubbyhole doors right and left. Grumbling to herself about how she was ruining her pretty pants—she'd crawled through grape juice in the first thirty seconds—she started getting more and more annoyed with every door she opened.

Of course, Mary Jo wasn't behind any of the doors, and Aimee's head was hurting again. "This is stupid," Aimee whined out loud.

Deciding that she was wasting precious time opening doors because Mary Jo was probably on the backside of the game, Aimee put her head down and just crawled at superspeed toward that area. She'd find Mary Jo there, for sure.

To get to the back of the game, Aimee had to pass the end of the main corridor. As she did, she glanced toward the entrance to see if anyone was waiting to play.

It looked like someone was. The grate was missing, and the entrance was open.

Aimee started to crawl on, but then she saw movement out of the corner of her eye. Turning, she nearly choked on her sharp inhale.

The man she'd seen in the arcade was peering in through the open entrance.

And he was looking right at her.

Frozen in midcrawl, Aimee could do nothing but stare at the man, who gazed back at her with the same wide grin he'd given Mary Jo in the arcade. The grin dropped Aimee's body temperature so fast that she felt like she'd just been flash-frozen. Every hair on her body bristled.

Aimee wasn't sure how long she and the man looked at each other. It felt like forever, but it was probably just a second or two. She didn't seem to be able to move.

But when the man stuck his head farther in through the game entrance, a movement that coincided with one particularly loud screech from the game soundtrack, her body decided it was time to get going. Aimee let out a little squeal and started crawling as fast as she could toward the exit.

That was it. She'd had enough. Forget finding Mary Jo. Aimee just wanted *out* of the Hiding Maze.

Aimee panted heavily and scrabbled noisily as she crawled the first several feet away from the main tunnel, but then she slowed and did her best to control her breathing. Trembling, she looked over her shoulder to see if the man was catching up to her.

She didn't see him.

But she heard him. At least, she thought she did. Even over the rain forest soundtrack, she could make out a few scuffles and thumps that seemed to be coming from the main tunnel. Forcing herself not to scream in terror, Aimee put her head down and started crawling again.

By the time Aimee was nearing the game exit, she knew more than three minutes had passed; it didn't matter what she did next. Mary Jo would be telling Aimee what to do for the rest of the day.

As if that was her biggest problem. The truth was that Aimee no longer cared what she did later today. She just wanted to get out of the game and get away from the creepy guy.

Seeing that creep again was the last straw. Aimee didn't want to be anywhere near Freddy's. She wanted to go home.

Twisting toward the game's exit, which also exited to the back alley of the building itself, Aimee checked over her shoulder to be sure the creepy guy hadn't followed her.

She didn't see anything. No one was behind her.

Aimee pushed the heavy wood door open. When the

fresh air hit her, she breathed it in and then exhaled in relief.

As she climbed out into the bright afternoon sun, though, she paused and looked back at the tunnel. Mary Jo was still in there. What if the creepy guy found her?

Aimee chewed her lower lip. She frowned. Finally, she shook her head.

No, he wouldn't find Mary Jo. She was hidden. It was much more likely he would have found Aimee, who was out in the tunnels.

Later, Aimee would explain to Mary Jo why she left. Mary Jo would understand.

Stringy hair falling over his dark, evil gaze, the creepy man reaches out and pulls on the cubbyhole handle. The door opens slowly, relentlessly, eventually revealing what it always reveals: Mary Jo, wide-eyed and pale. Launching herself at the man, Mary Jo screams and scratches at his bare arms. She's a fighter, and she's not going to let him take her easily. But Mary Jo is no match for the man's strength. He clamps her arms to her sides and drags her from the cubbyhole as Mary Jo screams what she always screams: "Aimee! Aimee where are you? Help! Why did you leave me?"

Aimee's eyes shot open. She rubbed them with trembling hands as she reoriented herself to wakefulness. Taking a ragged breath, she realized where she was. She'd been studying, and she'd fallen asleep.

Even though sun splayed over the beanbag chair where Aimee was curled up in the corner of her dorm room, she felt chilled. She always felt chilled after that dream.

Aimee hugged herself, rubbing her arms to try to warm up. *Face it*, she thought, *you're not going to be able to read today.*

She never could read on this day.

This sunny day in mid-May might not have been a day that meant anything to anyone else, but to Aimee, this day had great meaning, just not "great" as in *good*. Aimee actually hated this date, and it never passed without her being aware of it . . . from the moment she got up in the morning to the moment she finally fell asleep at night, which generally didn't happen until she'd done a lot of staring at the ceiling and even more tossing and turning.

Aimee sighed and dropped her book. What was she thinking, trying to read a book on the future of corporate economics on a day like today?

Stretching her legs, Aimee stood and wandered over to the window that looked out over the quad below. She twirled a few strands of her long hair, watching a couple guys she knew play Frisbee. They were good; the disc flew low and straight over the top of a couple dozen sun worshippers and last-minute studiers, and it never hit anyone. Aimee smiled and took a deep breath. This would be the last week she'd have this view.

Graduation was in a week, and three weeks after that, she'd be starting the new job she already had lined up. Before she did that, though, she was going to have to do something she'd been thinking about doing for a long time. There was no doubt in her mind now. She had to do it, if she ever wanted to be free from her past. She'd carried this weight around for ten years. That was long enough.

Turning away from the window, Aimee walked over to her neatly made bed. She sat and stared at the bare mattress on the other side of the room.

Aimee's roommate had finished exams the previous day, and she'd already packed up and gone home. Her boyfriend was back home, so she'd planned to spend the week with him, and then return for commencement. Aimee didn't have a boyfriend at home—or here at college, for that matter—and she had two more exams still to take. She just hoped she could concentrate well enough not to screw up her grade point average . . . but Mary Jo might make that impossible.

Mary Jo.

Did anyone else ever think about the frizzy-haired eleven-year-old who'd always thought rules were meant to be broken? Probably not.

Aimee shifted so she could see herself in the full-length mirror beside her dresser. She'd seen photos of herself at eleven years old, and she didn't think she looked a lot different now. She was small and skinny then, and she was petite and slender now. Obviously, her face looked a little different because now she wore makeup, but the slight slant of her eyes and severe arch of her brows, the upturned nose, and the slightly pouty mouth were the same. In the photos she'd seen of her younger self, Aimee's long blonde hair had usually been held back in a ponytail or a braid. That was still how she wore her hair.

What would Mary Jo look like now? Would her hair

still stick out from her head? Would her smile still be as big?

At first, Aimee liked to tell herself that she never saw Mary Jo again after that day in the Hiding Maze because Mary Jo got mad and ran away. It was a reasonable conclusion. Mary Jo had often threatened to run away, and she'd always had that backpack with her, ready to go.

But years later, when Aimee was being honest with herself, it was pretty clear that Mary Jo hadn't *run* anywhere. Aimee's dream told her that. The reoccurring dream—no, not a dream, her *nightmare*—had been telling Aimee the truth for ten years.

Aimee pulled away from her reflection and lay back on her bed. She forced herself to travel into the past.

As she had done literally thousands of times now, Aimee tried to convince herself there was no way she could have known something bad would happen to Mary Jo when Aimee left the Hiding Maze. Even though she'd been afraid of the creepy guy, Aimee's eleven-year-old mind hadn't really believed he found Mary Jo and hurt her. And since then, she'd tried very hard to believe that Mary Jo was never seen again because of something else, something that had nothing to do with what Aimee did.

But in truth, Aimee knew she was, in part, responsible. Just in part, though. The *true* culprit was the creep Aimee had seen in the arcade and at the entrance of the Hiding Maze right before she left it.

The evening of the day she'd last seen Mary Jo, Aimee had also seen the creep on TV. He'd been arrested for the attempted kidnapping of some other kid. She didn't normally pay attention when her parents watched the news, but she'd seen the guy's face, and she'd heard his name, Emmett Tucker. She'd also heard the word *kidnapping*. When she'd heard that word, her stomach had turned into a rock that dropped all the way to her feet.

When it was clear Mary Jo had disappeared, Aimee just *knew* that creep had taken her friend. He'd taken her, and he must have killed her. Apparently, the police were never able to prove that he did, so the guy went to prison just for the attempted kidnapping of the other kid. Aimee took some comfort in that, but not knowing exactly what had happened to Mary Jo ate away at her.

For years after Mary Jo disappeared, Aimee had carried guilt like a backpack even heavier than Mary Jo's. She'd known the creepy guy was poking around the Hiding Maze, and she'd left her friend there. She was sure Emmett Tucker had taken Mary Jo, and it was Aimee's fault.

Just a few months after Mary Jo disappeared, Aimee and her family had moved to another state. Long before the time they'd left—actually, just a couple weeks after the last time Aimee saw Mary Jo—the Freddy's where Aimee and Mary Jo had played in the Hiding Maze had closed. Aimee was never sure why. Her mother thought Freddy's closed because it was "inherently unsafe" for children; she'd never thought the animatronics were a good idea. Aimee's mom was very upset that the town they moved to also had a Freddy's. She didn't have to worry, though. Aimee never went to it. It reminded her too much of Mary Jo.

But last week, her mom had called her, interrupting the cramming Aimee was doing for her Commercial Transactions class. Stepping out of the library and into the cool night to take her mom's call, Aimee had looked up at the stars as she'd said with a sigh, "I'm studying, Mom."

"I know you are, sweetie. But I just wanted to check in on you. How's it going?"

"Fine, Mom. But I do need to concentrate."

"I know. I know. I just thought you could take a break and chat for a few minutes." Aimee's mom's smooth and deep voice broke into a chuckle. "You know, a few seconds for your dear old mom."

Aimee sighed. Through the phone, she could hear footsteps tapping on hardwood floors. She could picture her mom pacing back and forth in the kitchen. That's what her mom always did when she was chatting on the phone. Aimee could see her mom's lovely face as if she was right here. Blonde and blue-eyed like Aimee but with more classical features, her mom had large eyes, high cheekbones, and a full mouth.

"Okay, Mom," Aimee said. "What do you want to chat about? You have two minutes. Go."

Her mom laughed. "Okay, I'll start the kitchen timer. Well, let's see. Your dad has taken up racquetball. It might be too much for him; his shoulders and arms are so sore he can barely lift his coffee cup."

Aimee smiled.

"Oh, and I saw a blurb on the news about that man we thought took Mary Jo. Remember him?"

Remember him? How could she not? Aimee felt all her

muscles contract at once, as they always did whenever she thought about Freddy's or Emmett Tucker. "What about him?"

"Oh, they let him out of prison. For good behavior, or some such nonsense. He's back in his home, free as a bird. For some reason, I've never forgotten him. Probably because of Mary Jo."

Aimee felt her stomach flip over and try to crawl up her esophagus. She thought she was going to be sick. Mary Jo's kidnapper was free?

"Aimee? Are you there?" her mom asked.

Aimee tried to talk, and the words caught in her throat. She swallowed and managed, "Yeah, Mom. Has he talked to the press or anything?"

"What? I have no idea. I just saw a little report about him is all."

"I have to go, Mom." Aimee practically threw the words at her mother. And she didn't wait for a response. She ran inside the library, straight to the bathroom, where she threw up. After sitting in the bathroom stall and crying for half an hour, she'd forced herself not to think about what her mom had told her. She had to study and take an exam.

But of course, she'd thought about it. She'd been thinking about it for a week now.

Even so, she'd made sure it didn't mess up her studying because before she went back to cramming the night her mom called, she made a decision. As soon as she graduated, she was going to go back to the town where she spent the first eleven years of her life. She was going back, and she was going to find out what Emmett Tucker did with Mary Jo.

Ten years of uncertainty couldn't turn into fifteen or twenty or more. Aimee could no longer live with the assumption that Mary Jo had been kidnapped by Tucker without proving that he really *did* kidnap her and finding out what he did to her friend. She needed to know where he put Mary Jo's body.

Aimee was tired of the nightmares and the horrible visions that played over and over in her head. She was also tired of trying to delude herself with the idea that Mary Jo had run off and was living happily ever after somewhere. She was going to discover and prove the truth once and for all.

Aimee remembered her hometown as a pretty little place. Hugging both sides of a river that flowed out of the nearby mountains, the town was the home of a billionaire who had built his corporation's headquarters here. The headquarters, designed to look like an old-time Western town, sprawled along the river on one end of town. That's where both Aimee's parents had worked. When the billionaire had a new complex, with a more modern design, built a few states away (probably so he could have a warmer place to visit in the winter), her parents were transferred. Aimee had never really grown to like the new state. Too hot for her. And she missed snow in the winters.

If it wasn't for Mary Jo—or actually, the absence of Mary Jo—Aimee would have probably applied for a job at the corporate headquarters here in her old hometown.

But she knew she couldn't handle living in a place that would remind her of her friend every day. Instead, she'd taken a job in a town a couple hundred miles from here. It had the same climate but no painful memories.

Aimee pulled her cute little red hybrid compact into the parking lot of the Riverside Motel just before sunset. When she turned off the engine, she tapped the steering wheel a couple times. Should she go now or wait until tomorrow?

She squinted up beyond the motel's redwood siding and river rock–covered pillars. A reddish sun was sinking toward the glacier-topped ridge to the west. Almost blood-red rays painted the white expanses. Aimee shivered. Tomorrow. What she needed to do could definitely wait until tomorrow.

Aimee looked away from the sunset. She turned and grabbed a bright-yellow sweater from the back seat. Slipping it on, she picked up her purse and got out of the car.

It took Aimee only minutes to check into the motel and find her room. Once there, she perched atop the beige coverlet on the queen-size bed. She was facing a mirror above the low pine dresser sitting against the exposed-log wall opposite the end of the bed.

"Well, here you are," she said to herself.

The mirror version of Aimee spoke at the same time she did, of course. Still, she had trouble recognizing herself. She looked older in this mirror, like she was pushing forty instead of barely getting to know twenty-one. Why did her complexion look so gray, her cheeks so gaunt?

Aimee raised a hand to her face and brushed a few strands of hair from her eyes. It felt like a stranger was touching her. How odd.

A tremor skittered down Aimee's spine, and she looked away from the mirror. She needed sleep was all. She'd studied hard for most of four weeks, and over the last three days, she'd partied just as hard. Aimee didn't have a ton of friends, but the ones she had were close ones. One of them, Gretta, was Aimee's closest friend since Mary Jo. She had superwealthy parents and lived in a mansion with a pool, tennis courts, a huge movie room, an equally large game room, and a massive ballroom. After exams were over, Gretta's parents threw Gretta and her friends a three-day party, complete with live music and food catered by the best chef in town. Gretta and Aimee had spent much of that time alone in the movie room binge-watching old romantic comedies. They both loved the quiet solitude. But they'd balanced it with plenty of swimming, dancing, and eating.

Aimee had been friends with Gretta since she and her parents had moved to the new state. She'd gone to junior high, high school, and college with Gretta.

Gretta was the opposite of Mary Jo, a much better match for Aimee than Mary Jo ever was. When Aimee had met Gretta, she'd realized that her mother's theory about friendship and balance had been a bunch of crap. Aimee and Mary Jo hadn't been friends because they balanced each other out. They'd been friends because Aimee had been too shy to tell Mary Jo to go jump in the river. Mary Jo had decided they were best friends, and Aimee had gone along with it. From that point on, everything had been all about Mary Jo. As long as they were together, they were doing what Mary Jo wanted. The only time Aimee had gotten to be herself had been when she was literally *by herself*.

Gretta had been the person who'd had helped Aimee figure this out. Gretta had just graduated with a BA in psychology, and she was going on to get a master's next. She wanted to be a therapist. Aimee was one of her unofficial practice patients.

Just the day before, as they'd floated in Gretta's parents' infinity pool, looking out over perfectly trimmed expanses of green lawn and pruned bushes, Gretta had said, "You realize that you don't need to find out exactly what happened to Mary Jo to get closure, right?"

Aimee, who had been sipping lemonade from a huge covered tumbler balanced on her flat belly, shook her head and smacked her lips at the tartness of her drink. "Yes, I do."

Gretta shook a headful of short curls. A stunning red-headed beauty with flawless pale skin, green eyes, and model-worthy features, Gretta was surprisingly unconcerned about her looks. She rarely wore makeup, and she cut her own hair, despite being able to afford the most expensive hairdresser in town. She wasn't particularly good at haircutting, so her curls were always asymmetrical.

"No, you *don't*," Gretta said. "The only thing you need to do is forgive yourself. That's it. Easy-peasy. One step. The end."

Aimee shook her head, and Gretta splashed water on

her. Aimee closed her eyes just in time, and after the water cascaded over her sweaty shoulders and arms, she kept her eyes closed.

With her sight taking a mini-vacation, Aimee's other senses stepped up. She could smell Gretta's coconut-scented sunscreen, the lemon in her own lemonade, and the chlorine in the water. She could hear the water, too; it lapped lazily against their floating loungers and splashed against the sides of the pool. From the tennis courts, the *thwack* of rackets hitting tennis balls drifted over. From even farther away, the soothing sound of horses' neighs reached Aimee's ears from the pastures.

Aimee took a deep breath, inhaling all this peacefulness. Then she said, "It's not as easy as you say it is. Mary Jo is missing because I left her in that game. I didn't warn her; I didn't tell an adult. I just left her right where that man could take her."

Gretta smacked the water with her hand. The sharp sound made Aimee flinch and open her eyes.

"God, you're so stubborn! How many times do I need to tell you that you don't *know* that?" Gretta asked. "You're not dumb enough to think that. You don't know what happened after you left. You don't know what she did after she left the game. Probably, some choice *Mary Jo* made led to her disappearance. *Your* choice had nothing to do with it."

"But Emmett Tucker—" Aimee began.

Gretta held up a hand. "Tucker Shmucker. You don't know for sure that he took Mary Jo and neither did the police. And if he didn't take her, then why is Mary Jo's disappearance your fault? I mean, I get it. You feel like your choice was responsible because it was such a *huge deal* for you. It's not Mary Jo's disappearance that marks that day for you; it's your standing up for yourself that makes the day so important. That was the first time you defied her, right? That's what you've always told me."

Aimee nodded.

She and Gretta had been through all this many times, but Gretta was right—Aimee was stubborn. It was hard to disconnect her act of defiance with the end of Mary Jo, and therefore it was hard not to blame herself for Mary Jo's disappearance.

"But I didn't really defy her," Aimee said. "Not directly anyway."

Gretta opened her mouth, and this time, Aimee held up her hand. "You make it sound like I was making this big self-empowering statement that day I left her in the game, but the truth is, I was just being a scared, petulant child. I mean, if I was going to actually stand up to Mary Jo, I would have told her no. I would have said, 'I don't want to play in the Hiding Maze. I'm going home to read.' I didn't do that. Instead, I did something that left her vulnerable, and now that Emmett Tucker is out of prison . . ." She shrugged.

"Because of that, you're filling your head with horrible images, imagining what he might have done to your friend, and you're heaping even more guilt on yourself. I know that the way you took your stand with Mary Jo was passive-aggressive, but you need to cut yourself some slack. You were *eleven years old*. Psychological mastery isn't a requirement for that age." Gretta winked at Aimee, and Aimee smiled.

"You're a good friend," Aimee said.

"So are you. And you were a good friend to Mary Jo. You owe her nothing."

Aimee twisted her lips.

Gretta sighed. "But you're still going back."

Aimee nodded. "I have to. I really do have to."

Gretta was quiet for several seconds. Inside the house, the band started playing again. So much for peacefulness. The bass was so strong it vibrated the surface of the water in the pool.

"I could still go with you. I meant it when I said I'd be happy to come," Gretta shouted over a screeching guitar riff.

"I know. But I need to do this by myself."

In her motel room, Aimee lay back on her bed as the image of her friend and the relaxing pool faded away. Now that she was here, she was really wishing Gretta had come with her. It would have been so much easier with Gretta along, maybe even fun. They could have turned it into a celebration of everything they had to look forward to in the coming years. They could have . . .

Aimee frowned and derailed that train of thought. This trip wasn't about having fun or celebrating. It was about finding out, once and for all, what exactly had happened to Mary Jo.

Aimee hadn't told her parents or Gretta exactly what she was planning to do. Aimee knew they would have tried to talk her out of it. She could just hear her mother telling her how dangerous the idea was.

But Aimee didn't think it was all that dangerous. Well, maybe a little. But she thought she could handle it.

Sure, when Aimee had been a little girl, Tucker was scary. But now? Aimee was more than capable of handling herself. She was strong and athletic, and she'd taken self-defense classes. Plus, she had both mace and a pretty blue Taser in her purse. And she had her determination. She was going to find out what Tucker did, one way or another.

Besides, Tucker was more than likely a wuss. He took little kids, not adults. He wouldn't know what to do with someone who could fight back. Or at least that was what Aimee told herself as she headed to Bernadette's Bakery on Main Street.

Before Aimee came back to face Emmett Tucker, she read the newspaper article about his release. The article had featured a photo of Tucker sitting in front of Bernadette's Bakery. A little research had revealed that though the bakery served tourists and locals alike, it was a favorite of longtime residents. Hoping Tucker was a regular, Aimee figured the bakery was a good place to start her search for him.

Bernadette's was one of a couple dozen long-established businesses in the heart of town. The little downtown area was built around a brick-covered square with a stone fountain and a rose garden, and Bernadette's was the shop closest to the fountain.

Aimee found a parking space two doors down from Bernadette's and got out of her car. Slipping her long purse strap over her head so the purse hung across her body, she pulled her sweater tight and headed toward Bernadette's pale-yellow storefront.

Several pigeons strutted back and forth in front of Bernadette's, snatching pastry crumbs from under the little metal tables on the patio. It was chilly this morning, and only a couple old guys sat at the tables.

When Aimee had arrived in town the previous evening, the sun had been setting in a clear sky. Today, the sun was taking a little vacation. A froth of gray clouds churned above the town like the balloons that had floated on the ceiling of Gretta's family's ballroom a couple days before. Those balloons, though, had been purple, not gray. And they'd promised happy times. The clouds overhead didn't seem to promise anything good. For some reason, Aimee found them ominous.

"Get a grip," she muttered to herself as she pulled open the bakery's bright blue door.

Bernadette's interior, thankfully, was warm, and it smelled of cinnamon, sugar, and coffee. Cramped and cute and frilly, the place didn't strike Aimee as one that would appeal to the likes of Emmett Tucker. She looked around to see if he was here. He wasn't, but she figured she might as well hang out a bit and see if he showed up.

The bakery's half dozen rickety wood tables were occupied mostly by plaid-attired locals, but a few stylishly dressed tourists were in the mix. Every table seat was taken, but a tall counter along one wall had a couple empty stools.

Aimee approached the service counter and waited

behind a tall woman ordering three dozen assorted pastries. While she waited, Aimee turned and watched out the window, her muscles tensed, her gaze darting around, scanning the street for Emmett Tucker.

Tucker didn't show up while Aimee watched, but he did eventually appear.

Aimee had been nursing a small latte and nibbling on a cinnamon roll for ten minutes, wondering if she was wasting her time. Maybe she should have gone to the county records office and tried to find Tucker's residence.

She was glancing at her watch for the fifth time when Bernadette's door swung open, and Emmett Tucker walked in.

Aimee knew Emmett Tucker had been in his early forties when he was arrested. He'd looked much older than that, but several things had contributed to the wrinkles that had cinched up his face. He'd apparently spent most of his adult life working outside, on construction sites, and he also was a chain-smoker. Aimee figured he probably ate junk food, too. He didn't look like someone who bought organic vegetables.

Now with his long hair gone, replaced by a buzz cut, Tucker was barely recognizable as the man he'd been when Aimee had seen him at Freddy's and on the news. But she knew him. Those eyes and those yellowed teeth were unmistakable. Sometime in the last ten years, Tucker had picked up a scar that bisected his left cheek, and he'd lost a few of his teeth.

No one greeted Tucker when he came into the bakery. The tourists didn't give him a glance. The locals flicked looks at him, but they quickly returned their attention to their coffee and rolls.

Tucker didn't seem to care one way or another about who was paying attention to him. He just ordered his coffee and cinnamon roll and headed back outside. Aimee half rose off her stool when he went out the door, but she sat down when Tucker settled himself at an outside table and proceeded to drink his coffee and eat his cinnamon roll as if it was a warm sunny day.

For twenty minutes, Aimee tapped her foot and sipped at the dregs of her cooling latte. Should she confront him now? That would probably be smart. But then again, maybe if she just followed him, she'd learn something about him that would make a confrontation unnecessary. She gritted her teeth. She should wait.

When Tucker finally rose from his table, Aimee stood and dropped her Styrofoam cup and paper plate in a trash bin by the door as she watched Tucker head north up the street. Before he could get out of sight, she exited the bakery and lingered by its tables as she watched Tucker angle off the sidewalk toward the driver's side of a faded old green van.

A van. *That* was suspicious. Didn't kidnappers use vans?

Aimee trotted quickly to her car and got in just as Tucker backed the van out of the angled parking spot in front of an art gallery. She quickly started her car and pulled out to follow him.

For the next hour, Aimee tailed Tucker to a pharmacy, where he picked up a prescription; to a gas station, where he put gas in the van; and finally to a grocery store, where he filled a cart with frozen dinners, chips, canned soup, cereal, and a gallon of milk. She was right about his lack of interest in organic vegetables; he didn't go anywhere near the produce aisle, period.

Aimee's heart rate had been fast and uneven when she'd started stalking her quarry, but by the time she got to the grocery store, it had settled down. It turned out that stalking wasn't all that interesting . . . at least not when your target was doing mundane things. It wasn't hard, either. At first, Aimee had been furtive. At the pharmacy, she'd hidden behind a display of sunglasses, and she'd even pretended to try on a few pairs so she'd have a "disguise." At the gas station, she'd pulled her car in behind a dumpster and gotten out to peer over the top of it while Tucker had pumped his gas.

In the grocery store, at first, she hid behind product displays at the ends of the aisles, but when it became obvious that Tucker was oblivious to his surroundings, she gave up the subterfuge and just followed him around. She did have a cart so she looked like a normal shopper, and she threw a little of this and a little of that in the cart, but she shouldn't have bothered. He never even looked her way.

After Tucker got back in his van in the grocery store parking lot, he headed out of town and turned onto a narrow rural road. She let a car get between her and Tucker just in case he'd noticed her—not that she thought he would; the town was filled with small hybrids similar to hers.

As she drove, Aimee kept her gaze on the roof of the van up ahead of her. It trundled along at a sedate pace, so it was easy to keep up.

At one point, a loud *caw* startled her, and she flinched when a crow swooped low across the hood of her car, barely avoiding her windshield. Rattled for reasons she didn't understand, she watched the crow fly up over a dormant cornfield.

Going this slowly, Aimee had plenty of time to survey her surroundings. The rural road was winding through the flatlands stretching out from the south side of town to the foothills of the distant mountains. A lot of this area was farmland, but she remembered there were a couple parks out this way, farther down the road. Along this stretch of the narrow, uneven road, though, neither farms nor parks were visible. Instead, dilapidated old mobile homes and deteriorating cottages with roofs succumbing to thick moss were surrounded by old cars up on cinder blocks and discarded furniture. Aimee spotted several broken trampolines, multiple rusting swings, and dozens of scattered toys left out in scruffy yards to be baked by the sun and drowned in the rain.

After about five minutes, Tucker's van slowed, and Tucker turned left next to a dented mailbox on a slanted wood post. Dust billowed up from the van's tires as he headed down a dirt driveway.

Aimee slowed and looked past the van. The driveway appeared to stop in front of an old mobile home. This must be where Tucker lived.

Aimee drove past the driveway and pulled off the road a couple hundred yards farther on. She parked on the road's gravel shoulder and looked back over her shoulder.

Yep. Sure enough. Tucker was unloading his groceries and heading toward the mobile home's front door.

Aimee slapped her hand on her steering wheel in celebration. This was her chance. She could finally confront him!

A tiny flutter in Aimee's belly might have been suggesting she was doing something that wasn't all that smart, but she ignored it. She didn't care about being smart right now. She cared about finding out what Emmett Tucker had done with Mary Jo.

Aimee did a tight U-turn on the narrow road. Returning to Tucker's driveway, she turned onto it.

Aimee's little car bumped through a pothole. She clenched her teeth and slowed the car to a crawl.

Peering through her now-dusty windshield, Aimee looked at her destination. A chill sluiced through her.

Maybe this wasn't such a great idea.

Emmett Tucker's home looked like it wasn't a fit place for rats, much less humans. Sitting in the middle of a small rectangle of bare dirt relieved only by the occasional wilted weed, the single-wide was either painted dark brown or it was so dirty it had become dark brown over time, and its windows were so caked with dust, they were barely recognizable as windows. Two of them were boarded over. The flashing around the base of the mobile home had long since torn away, and the rusted wheels of the home's undercarriage could be seen balancing on crumbling cinder blocks.

Reaching the barren earth in front of Tucker's home, Aimee did another U-turn and parked her car with its front end pointed toward the road. She wanted to be in position for a quick getaway if need be.

Glancing in her rearview mirror to see if Tucker had come back outside (he hadn't), Aimee grabbed her purse and got out of the car before she could change her mind.

Looking up at the dark sky, she slung her purse across her body. She unsnapped the purse and kept her hand inside, tightly grasping her Taser. Then she pointed herself toward Tucker's front door and marched over to it with her chin lifted and her shoulders set.

She was just stepping up onto the rotting porch when the black-painted front door swung open. She stuttered to a stop and forced herself not to backpedal. She looked into the eyes of the man she'd seen in Freddy's ten years before.

"Whatever you're sellin', I'm not buyin'," Emmett Tucker said. Up close, he looked even worse than he had in the bakery. His skin was so thin you could see his veins crawling under the surface.

Aimee didn't want to be here any longer than she had to be, so she got right to the point. Clutching her mace and planting her feet, she recited her prepared lines.

"Ten years ago, my friend Mary Jo and I saw you at Freddy's. That was the same day you were arrested. It was also the same day Mary Jo disappeared. I want to know what you did with her."

Tucker blinked once and leaned against the doorjamb. Slowly, he reached into the sagging pocket of his baggy jeans. Aimee stiffened and tightened her grip on the Taser.

Tucker pulled out a pack of chewing gum and

methodically unwrapped a piece. Folding it into his mouth, he tossed the wrapper onto the porch. "I quit smoking," he said.

"Good for you," Aimee said without thinking.

Tucker leaned back and gestured toward the interior of the mobile home. "Wanna come in?"

Aimee bit back her "Hell no," and said politely, "No thank you. I'm fine out here." She swallowed. "I realize you probably won't answer my question. Why should you? You never admitted to anything before. But I had to come and ask. I had to."

For several seconds, Tucker chewed his gum loudly. The sucking and smacking sounds made Aimee's skin crawl.

Then Tucker took a step forward. Aimee backed away quickly.

Tucker chuckled at her, then gestured at the porch step. "I tell you what. You sit here with me, all neighborly like, for a spell, and I'll answer your question."

Aimee frowned and looked at the porch. She glanced back up and saw that Tucker's gaze had dropped from her face to her fitted scoop-neck pale blue top and on down to her tight navy-blue pencil pants.

Aimee kept her expression neutral. She didn't like being stared at . . . by anyone. She didn't like it, but she'd learned to ignore it. She wasn't going to let Tucker intimidate her. She looked down at the porch again. She realized she was inspecting it for some kind of hidden trap. Why did he want her to sit with him?

She shrugged. Okay. If that was what it was going to take.

"You first," Aimee said, gesturing at the step.

Tucker chuckled again and sank down onto the splintered wood planks. Aimee followed suit, positioning herself out of his reach. She kept her grip on the Taser.

For several seconds, they sat in silence. In the distance, a dog barked once. A truck rumbled past on the road. The breeze picked up, and the sky seemed to lower even more.

"Well?" Aimee said.

Tucker turned to look at her. "I remember you. You and that girl everyone thought I took were in Freddy's that day."

Aimee forced herself not to shiver.

Tucker cocked his head. "You were the one I saw in that tunnel thing when I was looking for my daughter."

Aimee could feel her pulse throbbing, double-time, at her temples. She kept her breathing even.

Tucker shrugged. "That's why I was there that day. I was looking for Jilly, my daughter. She always liked going to that place."

He turned abruptly and shifted closer to Aimee. She pulled her mace halfway out of her purse, but she didn't lean back. Instead, she looked directly into Tucker's eyes. "And where did you take my friend?"

Tucker chewed his gum and held Aimee's gaze for several seconds. Then he shook his head. "I never took *any* kid. All's I was trying to do when I got arrested was get my *own* kid back from that lying tramp I married. So what if she got custody? Why does a court get to decide who gets custody of a man's daughter? That judge had *no business* giving my girl to my ex. It was my *right* to have my own kid. I was just standing up for my rights! I never shoulda been sent to prison for that!" Tucker pounded his fist on the porch, and Aimee jumped up.

"You're lying!"

Tucker scowled at her. "Who the hell are you coming to my home and telling me I'm lying?"

He stood, and Aimee took a step back.

"Get out of here!" he shouted at her. "I've had enough of folks thinking I did stuff I didn't do!"

"Tell the truth!" Aimee yelled. "You took Mary Jo. I know you did! She yelled at you, and so you took her! You took her, and you killed her!"

Tucker's face flushed red. "Why the hell would I care if some little snot kid yelled at me? I didn't take your stupid friend! And I ain't never killed anyone!"

Aimee pulled out her Taser and aimed it at Tucker's chest. "Tell me the truth, or I'll tase you!" All the anger and frustration and guilt she'd hung on to for ten years came out in the screeched words and spittle that flew from her mouth.

Tucker jerked forward and reached for the Taser. Aimee didn't hesitate. She pressed the button.

Tucker whipped his body away so the Taser missed him. When it did, he started cussing. "What the hell's wrong with you?" he bellowed. He swung out at her.

Aimee zigged away from his blow and then stepped in before he could swing again. Furious, she kicked him in the shin.

"Ow!" Tucker glared at Aimee, bent over, and charged at her.

Feeling pleased with herself for hurting Tucker, Aimee wasn't ready for Tucker's move. She tried to avoid him, but he grabbed her. She screamed and attempted to slip a hand into her purse to get her mace. But Tucker had her in a bear hug, and he tightened it. Then he lifted her off the ground.

"Crazy girl!" he growled at her as he backed toward his open front door.

"Let me go!" Aimee spewed as she flailed in Tucker's grip. She tried to remember her self-defense moves. What was she supposed to do when someone held her tight like this?

Her heart pounding, sweat trickling down her spine, Aimee remembered. She threw her head up, trying to whack Tucker's chin.

All she did was whap her forehead into his chest. She was too short to do him any harm that way.

By this time, Tucker was carrying her inside his dingy home, and Aimee's fury was turning into fear. She writhed this way and that, but she couldn't break lose. So, she started to scream.

"Shut the hell up!" Tucker shouted. He carried her past a filthy kitchenette and into a tight dark hallway that smelled like dirty laundry and cooked sausages.

Aimee picked up her feet and tried to kick at the walls, but the space was too cramped. She screamed again, and Tucker kicked a small door open and tossed her through the opening. Aimee's hip hit the corner of a miniature bathroom cabinet, and her head flew forward and hit a small mirror. Wincing, she struggled for her balance and turned to face Tucker . . . just as he slammed the door.

"I'm calling the police!" Tucker yelled through the cheap wood.

"Good!" Aimee yelled back. "You should be in prison!"

"I'm not the one going to prison," Tucker shouted. "You assaulted *me*!"

Aimee opened her mouth to yell a response, but then she realized he was right. But it was self-defense, wasn't it? Of course it was. She'd tased him because he'd reached out at her.

Reached out. Okay, so maybe that wasn't enough for her to claim self-defense.

But he was a kidnapper!

Yeah. Of kids.

Aimee rubbed her sore hip and tried to steady her breathing. It refused to steady. She was taking heaving gulps of air. Through the door, she could hear Tucker talking on the phone. She caught the words *crazy girl* and *assault*.

She shook her head and frowned. She couldn't let the police get involved in this. They might arrest her. And even if they didn't, she'd waste all kinds of time trying to get it all straightened out. No. She had to get out of here.

Aimee reached out and tried the doorknob. Locked. Not a surprise. She thought about throwing herself at the door, but she quickly dismissed that idea and turned to look at the room.

She was in a minuscule bathroom, a very disgusting bathroom with toothpaste drying on the sides of the sink, a brown ring around the grayish tub, and stains she didn't want to think about on the floor around the toilet. But the bathroom did have a window above the toilet. It was small, but so was she.

Cringing, Aimee gingerly put the toilet lid down and climbed onto it. Unlatching the window, she shoved it open and levered herself up onto its narrow ledge. She stuck her head through the opening and pushed off the toilet lid.

The window's metal sides scraped at her shoulders as she squirmed forward. She heard her sweater snag and rip, but she kept going. She pushed through and looked down. A dead bush squatted under the window. She figured it would break her fall, so she slithered farther and let herself drop to the ground.

The bush did break her fall, but it also scraped her hands and arms. It hurt, but Aimee kept her teeth clamped together. Breathing hard, she glanced up at the window to be sure Tucker wasn't coming after her, and then she tore around to the front of his mobile home.

As she did, she heard a siren in the distance. She ran faster.

Jumping into her car, Aimee had the engine started when she saw, in her rearview mirror, Tucker barreling out of his mobile home. She quickly put the car in gear, and it shot down his bumpy dirt driveway.

Aimee passed a police cruiser just a few hundred yards after she got back onto the road. She made sure she drove sedately and looked innocent as it went past. Once it did, she sped up.

Her hands and arms stinging from the scratches the bush gave her, her hip and head sore from being tossed into the bathroom, Aimee was literally shaking. She felt beat up and freaked out. Whether she was shaking in pain, anger, or relief she didn't know. She made herself take long, even breaths as she kept glancing in her rear-view mirror to be sure no one was pursuing her.

Aimee ground her teeth. She slapped her hand on the steering wheel, *not* in celebration this time. She fisted her hand and pounded on the steering wheel in frustration.

How had this gotten so turned around? Tucker was the criminal. Not her!

Tucker was more than likely giving the police Aimee's description and a description of her car right now. She should probably get out of town.

The thick gray clouds that had been hovering so low all morning finally gave up trying to hang on to their moisture. Fat raindrops smacked at Aimee's windshield.

But was that it? Would she never find out what had happened to Mary Jo?

Aimee realized she was feeling more than beat-up and freaked out. She was devastated.

"What were you expecting?" she asked.

Had she thought Tucker would admit to taking Mary Jo and tell her he would have taken Mary Jo no matter what Aimee had done? Had she thought she was going to get a big old "It wasn't your fault" speech from the man?

She realized she wasn't sure what she'd expected from her conversation with Emmett Tucker. But now . . . well, now she was left with even more questions than she'd lived with for ten years. If he wouldn't admit to what he did, how was she going to find out what had happened to Mary Jo?

"Seriously, how do I prove what he did?" Aimee asked the heavier rain, now streaking across the glass in front of her.

Should she just leave? Should she do what Gretta was always saying—go into therapy, learn to forgive herself, and forget about Mary Jo?

Aimee shook her head. She couldn't do that. Any of it. She didn't want to go into therapy. She didn't want to leave without finding out something. And she couldn't forget Mary Jo. Ever. Mary Jo deserved to be remembered.

So, what other options did she have?

Aimee looked past the rain to the town ahead. The answers to her questions had to be here someplace.

The rain picked up even more. Aimee reached out and turned up the speed of her windshield wipers. The *swish-thunk-swish-thunk* rhythm of their swipes across the glass was strangely comforting.

"I can do this," she said, pressing harder on the accelerator and concentrating on her slow breathing. She was going to figure out once and for all what happened to Mary Jo.

And she knew just where to go next. She was going to do what all detectives did: return to the scene of the crime.

Aimee kept breathing slowly and deeply until she pulled into Freddy's crowded parking lot and . . .

Hang on a second.

Aimee frowned at the sprawling two-story building at the edge of the lot. It was in the right place. But that was about it. This wasn't Freddy's.

Aimee glared at the massive building that appeared to have eaten Freddy's, and as she looked at it, she realized it *was* Freddy's. It was just an abominable version of Freddy's. The old pizzeria had been built over and around, bloating it into what looked like a kitschy tourist trap.

With two stories instead of Freddy's one, this restaurant looked to be entirely new. It was rustic in appearance, but that was a facade. Its faux-old-timey siding looked too pristine and clean to have been around for long.

Aimee ducked her head to look out and up through her windshield at a big wood sign supported by a couple of tall, thick logs. Burned into the blond wood, black letters spelled out the name of the restaurant now occupying Freddy's old building: FLO'S FABULOUS EATERY. Under the sign, a smaller dark green sign with white lettering read, HOME OF THE LEANING TOWER OF PANCAKES. COME ON IN, AND SIT A SPELL.

A car engine revved nearby, and Aimee was jolted back to the present. She sank low in her seat. Had the cops found her?

Behind her, a big black truck backed into a nearby parking slot. She blew out her pent-up air, slid forward in her seat, and checked her appearance in the mirror on her visor.

Amazingly, she didn't look like she'd just been in a confrontation. Her hair was mussed, but it went back into place when she finger-combed it. Her face looked fine. The backs of her hands were scratched, and there was a little blood on the sleeve of her torn sweater, but it wasn't all that noticeable. She'd pass inspection if no one looked at her closely.

Aimee flipped up her visor. She'd better get inside and look around before she was spotted.

Checking over her shoulder for the third time since she left her car, Aimee stepped into the lobby of Flo's Fabulous Eatery. It was just after noon, which explained why the clatter of utensils and buzz of conversation coming from the restaurant's dining room was loud.

Aimee nearly jumped out of her shoes when she was greeted by an effervescent woman about her own age. "Welcome to Flo's Fabulous Eatery!" the woman said. "Did you bring your hunger with you?"

Aimee tensed, and then, forgetting her predicament for a second, she blinked and stared at the woman who'd spoken to her.

The woman laughed. "This must be your first time here. I know. I look ridiculous. Flo isn't a person. She's a cow." She pointed. Aimee turned and widened her eyes at a life-size sculpture of a Holstein cow. It was right inside the restaurant doorway, but Aimee had missed it because she'd been focused on what she was here for.

Aimee turned back to the hostess and gestured at the black-and-white cow costume the woman wore. She focused on keeping her tone light and innocent. She was just a diner here for a meal. She was *not* a fugitive investigating a disappearance. "Well"—she read the woman's name tag—"Kim, you make Holstein look good."

Kim—olive-skinned with big brown eyes and wavy brown hair—did actually look kind of cute in the costume. It helped that she had a dimpled smile. She wasn't taking herself too seriously. "Thanks!" she said. "You're very nice." She picked up a menu and turned toward the dining room.

Aimee hesitated, looking around to check if anyone was observing her. No one was. She glanced at the decor.

Aimee had hoped that once she was inside the restaurant, she would see something familiar. But nothing was as she remembered it.

Freddy's lobby had been large but mostly empty, just lined with red benches to sit on when you had to wait for a table. An archway had separated the lobby from the huge dining room. From that archway, you could see the stage and the animatronics.

Flo's lobby was even bigger than Freddy's had been, and it was filled with furniture, set up to look like a sitting room in a nineteenth-century home. It held at least a dozen overstuffed settees, ottomans, and chairs. Instead of an archway leading into the dining room beyond, what looked like the gates to a pasture separated the waiting area from the eating area.

Even from here, through the slats of the "gates," Aimee could see that the dining room was totally different than it had been when the building had been a Freddy's. For one thing, the stage where the animatronics used to perform—which should have been on the far side of the dining room—was gone. For another thing, the black-and-white tile floor had been replaced with a bright-green linoleum floor. She thought that was weird—the black-and-white floor would have fit right in with the Holstein cow theme. But maybe the green floor was supposed to be grass or something. It probably was, given that Freddy's red-painted walls had been covered over by murals depicting farmland and meadows filled with wildflowers.

Aimee flashed back to entering Freddy's when she was a kid. Besides the floor and the stage and the animatronics, the other thing she'd always noticed first was the carnival-like music and bells and jingles of the arcade games—that and kids screaming and laughing and running all over the place. Flo's had nothing like that. All Aimee could hear now was classic country music playing from speakers overhead and the normal clinks and clatters and chatter of families dining. She did hear a few kids giggling, but she didn't see them.

"I know the place is a little cliché," Kim said, "but the food's really good."

Aimee stiffened and looked at Kim. "What?"

Behind her, the restaurant's door opened. She glanced toward it, holding her breath. But it was just an older couple wearing matching pastel jackets. Not the police.

Kim smiled. "I was telling you the food's good, in spite of how the place looks." She gestured at the lobby. "The owners were farmers before they bought this place, and they're really into cows—their history and such."

Aimee nodded, her lips pressed together. She wished she could just slip away and poke around, but Kim said, "Follow me."

Aimee had little choice but to comply. Still on edge, she trailed Kim through the fake gate and on into the packed dining room. Aimee was still looking for evidence of the old Freddy's. Maybe the booths? She looked around. Nope. Flo's did have booths, but they weren't red like the ones in Freddy's. They were brown vinyl, made to look like branded leather. The dividers between the booths were different, too—they were made of reclaimed barn wood that stretched nearly to the ceiling.

Kim led Aimee to a booth at the far-left side of the dining room, in the area that used to be Freddy's arcade. Aimee took a seat and tried to remember what had been in this spot ten years before. Maybe the air hockey table? Or had it been a pinball machine?

Aimee accepted a menu, encased in heavy faux leather, from Kim.

"Your server will be Mary. She'll be with you in a minute. Enjoy your meal."

Aimee barely managed a nod and a smile because when Kim had said, "Mary," a chill had rushed through Aimee's body. It was so intense that she had to clench her teeth to keep them from chattering.

Mary. What were the odds of being served by someone with a name similar to Mary Jo's?

"Probably not that huge," Aimee whispered to herself. *It's just a coincidence*, she thought.

"Hi, I'm Mary," a middle-aged woman with died spiky red hair and too much makeup said. "How are you doing today?"

"Oh, you're not a cow," Aimee said. As soon as she

said the words, she realized how they'd sounded, and she flushed. "I mean . . ."

Mary barked out a deep, rough laugh. "That depends on who you talk to." She laughed harder.

"I'm sorry," Aimee said, putting a cool hand to one of her hot cheeks. She really needed to calm herself and focus. "I was referring to—"

"The costume. I know." Mary looked down at her Holstein-patterned apron, which she wore over black pants and a black blouse. "Servers get away with just this." She gestured at it. "When the place first opened, they apparently tried to put the servers in the cow costumes, but being a hostess in that getup is totally different than trying to wait tables in it. They figured that out quick."

Aimee nodded.

"So, what can I get you to drink, sweetie?"

"A cola? Whatever you have."

"One cola coming up. I'll give you some time to look at the menu."

"I also need to use the restroom," Aimee said. She didn't, but she wanted a chance to poke around. "I, um, may need several minutes."

"No problem."

"Thanks."

"The restrooms are through that door," Mary said. She pointed toward what used to be the back of the arcade area at Freddy's.

"Thanks."

As soon as Mary walked away, Aimee slipped out of the booth. She still had her bloody, torn sweater on, and she still had her purse slung across her body. She wasn't sure if she actually was going to stay to drink the soda she'd just ordered. It depended on what she found when she went looking.

Standing and checking to see if anyone was watching her (no one was), Aimee walked quickly past a back exit from the restaurant, on toward the hallway leading to the restrooms. She idly noticed that a cobweb blew out from a vent at the base of the wall on the left side. Passing its dancing filaments, she entered the hall. Once there, she bypassed the doors marked LADIES and GENTS. She didn't think there would be anything to find in new bathrooms. But there was a door marked MAINTENANCE at the back of the hall that was promising; it was in the area where the entrance to the Hiding Maze used to be. If there was anything left to indicate what had happened to Mary Jo, it would be there.

Or at least, that was Aimee's theory.

Not that she was too excited about her theory.

Ever since she'd entered Flo's Fabulous Eatery, her enthusiasm for her return to the crime scene plan had waned . . . a lot. She wasn't sure what she'd been expecting. Obviously if the restaurant looked totally different on the outside, it would be totally different on the inside, too. Had Aimee really thought she was going to find a clue in a place that had been completely and totally remodeled?

"Just get on with it," Aimee told herself. She was here; she might as well poke around.

Checking over her shoulder to be sure she was still

alone, Aimee hurried to the end of the hall and put her hand on the knob of the door marked MAINTENANCE. Would it be locked?

She turned the knob. Not locked. The door opened right up. Looking behind her one more time, Aimee slipped into the dark room and pulled the door closed before she started feeling the wall for a light switch.

The room smelled of musty cardboard, bleach, and lemon-scented cleaners, and it felt chilly and damp. The closed door muted the sounds coming from the dining area, so it was nearly silent in the room. The only thing Aimee could hear clearly was the sound of her own rapid breathing.

After several seconds, Aimee still hadn't found the light switch. In those seconds, her imagination had conjured up all sorts of things that could have been skulking in the dark, waiting to leap out at her before she got the light on.

After Aimee and her parents had moved to their new home, all of Aimee's new friends had loved horror movies and ghost stories. In the summer, her parents sent her to camp, and one of the favorite activities there was hanging around a bonfire in the dark listening to scary stories. Aimee had hated those stories. To fit in, she'd sat there with her friends, but she'd done her best not to listen. Instead, she'd hummed in her head. When Gretta and her other friends dragged her to horror movies, she'd sat with her eyes closed . . . and hummed in her head.

She was humming in her head now as she began scrabbling frantically for the light. She'd been in the unlit space long enough. She felt prickles between her shoulder blades, as if her body could sense the spot where a hidden person wanted to plunge a knife.

"Where is the light switch?" Aimee hissed as she kept pawing at the wall on either side of the door.

She was about to give up and go back out into the hallway when she heard footsteps entering the hallway outside the door. She froze. Was she about to get caught?

Backing away from the door, Aimee tried to think of what she'd say if someone found her in here. Nothing besides "I was looking for the restroom" came to mind, and that excuse would only work if she could convince whoever found her that she was blind. Only a person who couldn't see could miss the oversize, cow-themed signs to the restrooms.

The footsteps in the hallway quieted, then stopped. The person must have gone into one of the restrooms.

Aimee exhaled the breath she hadn't realized she'd been holding. She stepped back to the door, which she could locate because of the light coming in underneath it.

She realized her eyes were adjusting to the dark. Whereas the room had seemed to be nothing but solid inky blackness moments before, now she could discern hulking shapes on either side of the door. She could also see what appeared to be a cord dangling down next to the door's trim. She reached out and pulled on it, hoping she wasn't yanking on something that would set off an alarm.

As soon as Aimee pulled the cord, the room was flooded with bright white light from a bank of fluorescent bulbs overhead. She immediately whirled in a circle to be sure that she'd imagined sharing the space with someone else. She had. She was alone.

The small room looked to be a combination of janitor's closet and storage closet. It had the same green flooring as the rest of the restaurant, and the walls were painted sky blue. A bucket and a mop sat in one corner, along with several brooms and dusters. Next to these, a shelf of cleaning supplies extended from the floor to the low ceiling. Next to that, another shelf full of paper products—paper towels, napkins, toilet paper—extended to the back wall.

Aimee looked at that far wall. It was partially obscured by a stack of boxes, but over the top of the boxes, Aimee could see what looked like the upper edge of a dusty vent cover. And above the vent cover, she thought she saw some faded orange and red paint. Was that part of the rainbow?

Her heart stuttered in her chest. Could it be? Was the Hiding Maze really still here?

Aimee quickly stepped forward and tried to shove aside the stack of boxes. It was too heavy to shove. Frowning, she pushed at the top box, which was above her head.

It wasn't too heavy on its own, so she lifted it up and set it aside. The one below it was even lighter. She moved it, too. She shifted one more box, leaving the two bottom ones.

Now that she'd moved the top boxes, she could see that she'd definitely found the entrance of the Hiding Maze game. The grate was dirty, and it looked a little rusty, but it was the right size and shape, and it was surrounded by the red, orange, yellow, green, blue, indigo, and violet of the old rainbow.

Aimee was surprised the new owners had left the grate and the rainbow. But then, the rainbow fit with the countryside theme of the place. They must have figured it went with the sky-blue paint. Or maybe they'd kept it as some kind of homage to the old pizzeria. She'd learned from watching her parents redo two old houses that if you didn't *have to* fix something, it saved money to leave it. Why move an old grate and paint over a rainbow in what was going to be a storage room?

The bottom two boxes were the heaviest ones, but now that she'd moved the others, Aimee could shove aside the remaining ones. She pushed them just far enough to clear a path.

Stepping up to the grate, Aimee grabbed its edge and pulled. It didn't move. She frowned. It hadn't been nailed shut or anything, had it?

She ran her fingers around the edges of the grate. No. It didn't feel like anything was holding it closed.

The sound of footsteps came from the hall again. They sounded different from the last footfalls Aimee had heard. These were heavier, slower. But they were coming closer.

Not willing to be caught now that she was so close to being able to investigate what she came here to see, Aimee quickly pulled back the boxes that had been blocking the grate. Positioning them just far enough from the grate to give her room to maneuver but close to where they had been when she'd come in here, she hustled to restack the other three boxes. She'd just put the last one on top when the door to the room opened.

Tucked behind the stack she'd just rebuilt in the nick of time, Aimee held her breath, this time on purpose. She listened as someone stomped into the room. She heard a soft shuffling sound and a heavy sigh, and then someone muttered, "And they yell at me for leaving the light on. Why should I turn it off if no one else will?"

More footsteps, moving away. The door closed.

Aimee took a deep breath and turned back to the grate. Maybe the rust on the grate was acting as a glue, holding the grate tight to the wall. Aimee frowned and tried tugging again.

She needed to hurry. She wasn't sure how long she'd been back here. Two minutes? Five minutes? More than that? How long would it take before someone came looking for her?

Aimee could feel tension pulling up her shoulders. Her neck felt stiff.

She stepped back from the grate and rolled her head in a circle. That brought a little clarity.

"Dummy," she said as she zipped open her purse.

Reaching into the small pouch, she pulled out a metal nail file. She may not have carried much in her purse, but she had the essentials.

She poked the end of the nail file between the wall and the rusty edge of the grate, and she worked it back and forth all along the top and part of the side. After just a minute or so, she felt something give.

Encouraged, she ran the file farther down the edge of

the vent, continuing to jiggle the grate with her other hand. It took another several seconds, but suddenly, the grate came away from the wall.

Aimee pulled it back fully. Holding it open, she ducked down to peer in through the opening.

The storage room's bright light landed on what Aimee had been hoping she'd find: the entrance room to the Hiding Maze game. It was still there.

Stretching out from the vent opening, the game tunnel disappeared into gloom, but the part Aimee could see was lined with fake trees and boulders and little wood cubbyhole doors. The doors looked like they were fuzzy with dust, as was the tunnel floor, but everything appeared to be intact.

It was obvious no one had been in the tunnel in years. *A lot of years.* Ten years, to be exact.

It wasn't just the thick dust that made that clear. Just a few feet inside the tunnel, the same sock Aimee had seen the last time she'd been here, lay crumpled. It had to be the same sock because it had a distinctive, multicolored stripe and a hole in the toe. Aimee looked beyond the sock, and spotted all the other debris she remembered from her last time in the game: the deflated balloon, the piles of confetti, and the broken red plastic fork.

Aimee felt her pulse quicken. Maybe no one had been in the game since it was last played. If that was so, she actually had a good chance of finding the clues she was looking for!

Aimee dropped down onto her hands and knees and crawled into the game entrance room. As soon as she was in it, the vent cover dropped into place behind her. Immediately, Aimee noticed that the dining room sounds were even more muffled. She could barely hear anything at all from the restaurant's eating area—just the occasional laughter, which sounded like it was miles away. She suddenly felt very, very alone.

"Calm down," she told herself. She turned around and sat cross-legged in front of the game console.

Whenever she'd used the console as a kid, it was always lit up. Now it was dark. Dark and dirty. It was covered with dust.

Aimee reached out and pressed a button at random, hoping it would light up if she did. For a few seconds, the console stayed dormant. But then, suddenly, the old Freddy voice Aimee remembered said, "Welcome to Freddy's Hiding Maze Hide-and-Seek Game. Please wait. A game is currently in progress."

Aimee turned away from the console. She started crawling down the tunnel.

As soon as Aimee started moving, dust wafted up around her. She sneezed, and her eyes started to itch. Resisting the urge to rub them, she kept going.

The old tree bark, hanging branches, and moss crumbled around her as they hit her. They were brittle with age.

Aimee was thankful that whoever had come into the maintenance closet had defied the rules and left the light on. The light was strong enough to illuminate most of the main tunnel. She could even see traces of the old chocolate frosting stains on one of the boulders.

She wasn't sure how well she was going to see after

she turned off the main tunnel, but Aimee wasn't too concerned about that. If she had to go back into the restaurant, eat a meal, leave to get a flashlight, and come back later, she would . . . as long as she could avoid being spotted by the police. But she couldn't leave now without at least doing an initial search for some sign of what had happened to Mary Jo.

Aimee took her time crawling down the tunnel because she was scrutinizing every inch of it. She wasn't sure what she was looking for. Signs of a struggle? Blood? A plea for help scratched into the tunnel walls? She'd thought about those kinds of clues whenever she'd thought about coming back to find Mary Jo. There had to be *something*. Tucker *must* have left behind something to prove he'd gotten into the game to take Mary Jo.

At the end of the first leg of the tunnel, where she'd be out of light if she kept going to the right or to the left, Aimee glanced at the other game console. This one was dusty, too, but it wasn't totally dark. Instead of a blank display like the one at the entrance had, this one could be read.

Aimee peered at it. Was that . . . ?

She crawled closer and rubbed her finger over the console's name display. She gasped. The breathy sound bounced around her, then faded away as she stared at the display.

The console panel still listed her and Mary Jo as the active players!

They were the last ones to play the game?

She hadn't known that.

Hoping that the game console and tunnel lights would come on, Aimee hit the RESET button on the console.

It worked! The console's display lit up. It was flashing FAILURE, but so what? What mattered was that the rope lights that lined the tunnels and surrounded the cubbyhole doors lit up.

Aimee grinned. "Yes!"

This would make her investigation easier. She started to turn away from the console so she could get on with it.

The rain forest soundtrack started playing, and Aimee shivered. Hearing the old rain sounds and screeches creeped her out.

She shook herself like a dog. She was being silly.

Aimee crawled away from the console and started to pass a closed cubbyhole. As she did, the slithery edges of a dark and horrifying suspicion started seeping into her consciousness. She pulled her head out of the cubbyhole and looked back at the game console, which was still flashing FAILURE.

Aimee plummeted from the sunny heights of the exultation she'd felt moments before into a low, slimy bog of dread. She turned and looked left and right down the tunnels that extended from the entry tunnel. Her gaze flitted frantically from one cubbyhole door to the next.

Her head pounding, Aimee turned right out of the main tunnel and started crawling faster, her gaze flitting frantically around her as she went. In spite of the chill in the tunnels, Aimee was sweating. She was also breathing hard. Her inhales and exhales were so loud that they echoed off the walls of the crawl spaces; it sounded like a pack of panting dogs was pursuing her.

After just a few minutes of crawling at a breakneck pace up and down through the tunnels and this way and that through the game's nooks and crannies, Aimee's knees began to protest what she was doing. Not used to repeated impacts on a hard surface, they began to pulse with burning pain. Her neck ached, too, because of the strained position she was keeping it in to look into each cubbyhole.

Aimee was circling back to the point where the first leg of the main tunnel intersected with the main passageways to the left and to the right. She glanced into an open cubbyhole, and she did a double take. Was that . . . ?

Aimee frowned and peered into the cubbyhole. She'd seen a flash of something red toward the back of the cubbyhole.

Crawling in through the open door, Aimee reached for what she'd seen. She couldn't quite grasp it, so she crawled the rest of the way into the cubbyhole just as her fingers closed over . . . her lost friendship bracelet. Wow. How weird was that?

Suddenly, Aimee's cubbyhole door swished shut, snapping into place. The tiny space went dim, lit only by the rope lights outside the cubbyhole. Their illumination just made it through the tiny window on the cubbyhole door.

"Hey!" Aimee shouted.

She twisted around so she could get the door open again. She whacked her head on the cubbyhole's wall. "Ow!"

Reaching out, Aimee tried to push the cubbyhole door open. It wouldn't open.

Outside the cubbyhole, Freddy announced, "Player Two has chosen a hiding spot! Player One, find Player Two! Go!"

"No, no, no!" Aimee shouted.

Aimee pounded on the door, but it still didn't open. Gulping in ragged breaths, Aimee shifted to shove her shoulder against the door. As she did, her face pressed up against the viewing window.

She looked out at the open door to the cubbyhole across from hers. Not much light fell into the cubbyhole from the rope lights, but the light that did make it revealed . . .

Aimee's breath caught, and then it released, along with a scream that contained every single particle of guilt she'd carried for the last ten years.

She now knew what had happened to Mary Jo.

"Player One, find Player Two," Freddy's voice ordered.

Sealed inside a cubbyhole for ten long years, Mary Jo's desiccated corpse had practically mummified. Curled inward, drawn down probably by the dried-up skin, Mary Jo's body was embracing her backpack, which she held like it was a baby. Had it given her any comfort? It didn't look like it had.

The skin drawn tight against her bones, Mary Jo's face was brown and leathery, frozen in what looked at first to be a rigid smile. Mary Jo's lips were gone, and her mouth was pulled back from her big teeth.

Whimpering, Aimee understood, of course, that Mary

Jo hadn't been smiling when she'd died. She'd probably been screaming, crying out for someone to hear her, to find her.

Aimee frantically shifted positions and kicked out at the door with both feet. It didn't do any good. She didn't have the room to pull her feet back far enough to get any power behind the kick. They just thumped the door ineffectually.

Outside the cubbyhole, Freddy nudged, "Player One, find Player Two."

Aimee pounded on her cubbyhole door again. She kicked at it over and over. She threw herself at it. It didn't budge.

Clearly, the game wasn't functioning right. The doors weren't going to open.

Aimee's heart crawled up into her throat. She began to hyperventilate, and she started begging, "Please, no!"

Once again, she pressed her face to the little window as if she could look for help. Nothing but Mary Jo's silent corpse looked back at her. Aimee threw herself at the door. It remained closed.

She started scratching at the edges of it. She dug at the rubber seal, trying to gouge it out.

Crying and wincing as her nails broke off, Aimee clawed and clawed. But the rubber seal remained impervious to her attack. It didn't even leave a mark on it.

Aimee sagged against the door. Sour-smelling sweat ran down her neck and trickled along her spine.

Surely someone would hear her eventually, wouldn't they?

They didn't hear Mary Jo, she thought.

Aimee began to tremble, and she forced herself to remain calm. It was going to be okay.

She wasn't like Mary Jo. People cared about her. Her parents would come looking for her. Her friends would look for her. Her car was in the restaurant's parking lot. Kim would remember her. Mary would remember that Aimee had asked where the restrooms were. They'd know she was in here.

But would they? Really?

No one knew the Hiding Maze was back here. Why would anyone look in an old crawl space for a missing woman?

Maybe they'd see the grate and—

"Find Player Two," Freddy's voice intoned.

Aimee lost all semblance of calm and gave in to panic. She started wailing, and then she shrieked. She shrieked until her throat burned and spasmed. And then she swallowed, and she screamed some more.

Aimee screamed until her lungs forced her to stop and fill them. Then she started crying. She sobbed at first, and then, thinking about her abandoned friend, she wailed.

Mary Jo had died the same way she'd lived, Aimee realized. She'd died because no one had cared enough about her to do whatever was necessary to take care of her.

"Find Player Two," Freddy's voice repeated.

Aimee pounded on the door of the cubbyhole and screamed at the top of her lungs.

★ ★ ★

Mary approached the nice young woman's booth and frowned at the soda sitting on the table next to the unopened menu. The soda clearly hadn't been touched. It was no longer fizzing, and at least half the ice had melted; a ring of condensation was pooling on the table's slick wood surface.

No one stayed in a restroom that long. The woman must have left.

Mary glanced up and saw Kim heading her way with an elderly couple in tow. Shrugging, Mary picked up the abandoned soda and menu, quickly wiped the table, and pointed at it. "You can seat them here, Kim. My last customer took off, I guess."

Kim smiled, nodded, and helped the couple get settled in the booth. As soon as Kim left, Mary grinned at her new customers. "Hi, I'm Mary," she said. "How are you doing today?"

From the vent near the hallway leading to the restrooms, an ever-so-faint scream reached out into the dining room. Its echo lingered for a couple seconds, but the sound was inconsequential.

It didn't stand a chance of being heard.

ABOUT THE AUTHORS

Scott Cawthon is the author of the bestselling video game series Five Nights at Freddy's, and while he is a game designer by trade, he is first and foremost a storyteller at heart. He is a graduate of The Art Institute of Houston and lives in Texas with his family.

Elley Cooper writes fiction for young adults and adults. She has always loved horror and is grateful to Scott Cawthon for letting her spend time in his dark and twisted universe. Elley lives in Tennessee with her family and many spoiled pets and can often be found writing books with Kevin Anderson & Associates.

Andrea Rains Waggener is an author, novelist, ghostwriter, essayist, short story writer, screenwriter, copywriter, editor, poet, and a proud member of Kevin Anderson & Associates' team of writers. In a past she prefers not to remember much, she was a claims adjuster,

JCPenney's catalog order-taker (before computers!), appellate court clerk, legal writing instructor, and lawyer. Writing in genres that vary from her chick-lit novel, *Alternate Beauty*, to her dog how-to book, *Dog Parenting*, to her self-help book, *Healthy, Wealthy, & Wise*, to ghost-written memoirs to ghostwritten YA, horror, mystery, and mainstream fiction projects, Andrea still manages to find time to watch the rain and obsess over her dog and her knitting, art, and music projects. She lives with her husband and said dog on the Washington Coast, and if she isn't at home creating something, she can be found walking on the beach.

"**B**low out the candles! Blow out the candles!" Jake's friends, wearing pointy cardboard party hats, surrounded him at the table. Right in front of him was a round, white-frosted cake decorated with nine rainbow-colored candles. Somehow Jake knew that the cake was red velvet with cream cheese frosting, his favorite.

Jake laughed at his friends' cheers, took a deep breath, and then huffed and puffed like the Big Bad Wolf in "The Three Little Pigs." He extinguished all the candles at once.

Jake's heart was full of happiness. There were smiling faces all around him, smiling faces that were soon to be stuffed with cake and ice cream.

But wait.

None of this was real. It wasn't even a memory.

Jake needed to wake up. He wasn't safe where he was in real life, and this dream had lured him into a false sense of security. And yet it was so tempting to stay where he was now, where everything felt so happy and cozy.

No. You have to wake up.

Larson had found his way out of the field. He wasn't sure that wandering the streets aimlessly was an improvement over wandering through a field, but at least the lighting was better and there was no danger of stepping in a cow pie. There had to be some way of getting out of whatever this weird space was and back into reality.

An idea popped into Larson's head. *Of course. The ball pit.* Maybe the ball pit where he had gotten the blood samples was the connection—the portal—that would bring him back to real life. As soon as he had the thought, it was like his feet automatically knew where to go. He walked several blocks despite none of the landmarks being familiar until he came to the site of the ball pit, Freddy Fazbear's, as it had been.

The place was hopping. Parents and children were spilling in and out of the doors, and even from the sidewalk, he could hear how loud the place was, the bleeps and blips of all the games, the music, the kids laughing and screaming with excitement. As soon as he entered the pizzeria, he could feel people's judgmental stares. It was weird enough for an adult man to come into a Freddy Fazbear's by himself, but it was even weirder when he looked as rough as Larson did. He was still bleeding from his injuries, and his white shirt was stained red. He was sweaty from his exertions, and he knew he stank. It was no wonder the patrons of Freddy's were giving him a wide berth.

But that was okay. He hadn't come here to make a good impression. He had come to find the ball pit.

And there it was. But it was a very different ball pit from the filthy one where he had collected the blood samples. This version of the ball pit was clean and new. The balls were bright primary colors, and the pit was full of laughing children, wading or "swimming" through the balls, sometimes throwing them at one another even though there was a sign saying you weren't supposed to.

"Police. I need everybody to get out of the ball pit, please," Larson said loudly enough, he hoped, to be heard over the games and music and voices. He wasn't, so he said it again, even louder and flashed his badge. This time the kids looked at him and made their way toward the ball pit's exit. Larson figured they were probably acting out of a desire to get away from him more than a wish to be obedient, but hey, whatever worked.

Larson climbed into the pit. He could feel the confused stares of kids and their parents. He relaxed his knees and let himself sink down until he was shoulder-deep in brightly colored plastic balls. Something about it felt like sinking into a bubble bath. But nothing about this was giving him any information that might help him get back to where he needed to be.

"I need to go farther down," he said to the onlooking parents and children. He wasn't sure why he felt the need to explain himself to them, especially when his words would only confuse them. He burrowed deeper into the ball pit until he was completely buried and surrounded by darkness.

Then, suddenly, it wasn't dark anymore. It was bright and sunny, and when Larson took a deep breath, his lungs filled with fresh air. He was walking down the sidewalk in a residential section of a pleasant town. The houses on the street were quaint bungalows, and the yards were well tended, with mowed grass and cheerful flower beds. The more he walked, the more familiar the town seemed. He suddenly remembered a newspaper clipping he had seen a while back. In a few steps, he saw something he definitely recognized from the clipping: a junkyard. Somehow he knew this was the place.

Once again, his feet led him as if they had exact knowledge of his needed destination. Inside the junkyard, Larson walked past piles of old tires and broken electronics and cast-off furniture until he came to an old, beaten-up car. Without even consciously thinking about what he was doing, he reached down and opened the trunk.

Eleanor leapt out in a fury, her jagged teeth bared, her hands shaped into claws. She pounced on him and knocked him down, scratching at him with her metal fingers, unhinging her jaws and snapping at his throat.

Eleanor was strong but also lightweight, so Larson managed to throw her off him and into a trash pile. He struggled to his feet just in time for her to come at him again, this time wielding a tire iron she had found. She swung it, and it connected with his jaw. For a second, he was blinded by pain. He was pretty sure she had loosened a tooth or two. He shook off the pain and managed to wrest the tire iron from her grip. He swung it hard and connected with her face, but she just laughed, a horrible, high-pitched cackle that made him shiver. He tossed away the tire iron. It was no use to him but definitely needed to be kept out of her reach.

Then he saw something a few yards away that might be useful, the trash compactor that was used to crush large metal items into smaller, more manageable cubes for disposal. He imagined Eleanor crushed to the form of a harmless cube, and almost smiled. He took off running in the direction of the trash compactor in hopes that she would chase him there.

"I've got something for you to chew on," he taunted her. "You stupid, useless doll!"

The heart-shaped necklace around Eleanor's throat pulsed and glowed blood red. Eleanor let out a horrible shriek—a warrior's cry—and charged at him. When she reached him, he grabbed her by the arm and shoved it into the waiting jaws of the trash compactor. Soon there were only the sounds of crunching metal and Eleanor's bloodcurdling shrieks.

Larson woke up lying on the floor in the house where he'd passed out. He looked up to see Eleanor still on the table. Her face was a mask of rage. In her anger, she was losing the appearance of the curly-haired girl and looking more like the deranged mannequin she really was. Her eyes were dark wells of anger.

"Renelle?" the man who thought he was her father said. "Renelle, what's happening to you?"

Eleanor opened her mouth impossibly wide. Gooey black tendrils shot from it, slithered across the floor, then twisted around Larson, binding him. The tendrils were sticky and smelled like copper. *Blood*, thought Larson. *They're made of blood.*

As soon as he thought this, he was back in the other place again, walking the streets. But this time he knew what to do. *The ball pit.* He had found Eleanor there before, and he would find her there again. And he would destroy her.

The former pizzeria was a dark, empty space with filthy, cracked windows. Strangely, the front door was unlocked, as if someone had been expecting him.

There were a few broken arcade cabinets and smashed-up tables and chairs. The walls had been covered with graffiti. But the ball pit was there in its regular place.

Larson stepped inside the pit. The plastic balls were sticky and adhered to his clothes and skin. They smelled of decay. He held his nose like he was jumping into a pool and sank beneath the surface.

Larson emerged into a dark room. Something metal brushed against his cheek; it felt like it could be the pull chain for a light fixture. He reached up and pulled it, and a bare, dim bulb cast a faint glow over the room. The walls were bare wood and sloped like the contours of a roof, and the room was cluttered with cardboard boxes and plastic tubs labeled WINTER CLOTHES,

CHRISTMAS DECORATIONS, and FISHING POLES/TACKLE. There was an old rocking chair and a table full of knickknacks—figurines, a large brass candelabra, a glass paperweight—the kind of stuff that nobody really needed but that people had a hard time letting go of for some reason. A large antique trunk sat in the far left corner of the room. Larson had a feeling that the trunk was hiding something other than useless bric-a-brac. With dread, he walked toward it.

Eleanor was lying curled up in the trunk with her knees hugged to her chest. Her eyes flew open.

She propelled herself out of the trunk and onto Larson, her cold metal hands encircling his throat. Larson grabbed her by the wrists, trying to loosen her grip, but she only grabbed on tighter. Choking and sputtering, he staggered backward, bumping into the table. He grabbed blindly at the table's surface and grasped the heavy glass paperweight. He raised it up and brought it down hard on Eleanor's forehead, rattling her enough to make her loose her grip on his throat.

Maybe paperweights weren't so useless after all.

She shook her head like she was disoriented, and then came at him again, this time with her jaw unhinged, exposing her sharp, jagged teeth. Larson grabbed the candelabra from the table and swung it hard, hitting her in the head and knocking her to the floor. He hit her face again and again, until the thin layer of sickly grayish skin was nothing but pulp, and the silver skull was exposed beneath.

Larson was on the floor in the house again. Looking

up, he saw Eleanor on the table. Her eyes were still closed, but her body was anything but relaxed. Her fists were clenched, her teeth gritted, and she shook her head back and forth as if she were saying *no, no, no*. Near Larson on the floor, the Stitchwraith had started to move, slowly scooting itself toward the table where Eleanor lay.

Larson blinked, and just like that, he was on the streets again. He knew what he had to do.

This time, the pizzeria was called Papa Bear's Pancake House. The windows were hung with red-and-white gingham curtains that matched the wipe-able plastic tablecloths. Only one table was occupied, with a family of four plowing through some pancakes. Near the coffee station, two servers in red-and-white gingham aprons chatted. He was relieved they hadn't noticed him yet. He looked in the back corner of the restaurant. Fortunately, the ball pit was still there, and the plastic balls were in a much more pristine state than they had been on his last visit.

He went under.

He was in a kid's bedroom—a little boy's, from the look of it. The comforter on the bed was light blue and decorated with race cars. A poster showing Freddy Fazbear and his friends hung on the wall over the bed. There were no kids around now, but the room brought Larson back to all those times he'd checked under Ryan's bed for monsters. He'd always told Ryan there was no such thing. He was wrong.

Larson sensed Eleanor's presence.

He dropped to his knees and lifted the bed skirt. Nothing.

He pulled back the floor-length curtains in case she was hiding behind them. Nothing there either.

But as soon as he saw the closet, he knew she was there. He opened the door, and a pair of metallic hands shot out, pulling him inside the dark, tiny space.

Eleanor grabbed Larson by the shoulders and slammed his head into the closet wall over and over until all he could feel was white-hot pain. He managed to jab an elbow into her belly, which knocked her off balance and freed him. He stumbled out of the closet and picked up an aluminum bat that had been stored with the other athletic gear. He dragged Eleanor out of the closet by her wrist, then swung the bat at her head like he was trying his best for a home run. The force of the blow knocked her head partially off, so it dangled crazily from her neck by just a few wires. Larson took another swing, this one even harder, which severed Eleanor's head entirely.

On the table, Eleanor was writhing as if in agony. The Stitchwraith had dragged itself all the way to the table and appeared to be trying to summon the strength to pull itself up to a standing position.

Larson was pounding the pavement again, already walking the well-worn path to the home of the ball pit. This time the restaurant was little more than a dark, empty hole with broken windows and graffiti. Most of what had been inside had either been stripped away or smashed.

But the ball pit was still there, dusty and dilapidated, the plastic balls covered with an unsightly gunk that had rendered them all the same indeterminate color. It smelled of rot and something worse. Larson breathed in and out through his mouth and tried to stifle his gag reflex. He went under.

The space was huge and cavernous. Moonlight streamed in from a skylight above. It looked like a warehouse of some kind, though it didn't seem to be storing anything these days. An old mattress and some sleeping bags in a corner suggested that someone could have made the place their temporary home. Larson looked around at the large, empty space. There weren't many places to hide.

Then he heard laughter, the high-pitched cackle that made the tiny hairs on the back of his neck stand up. It was coming from above him.

She was peeking through the open skylight.

She dropped downward, landing on Larson, knocking the wind out of him. He lay flat on his back.

Jake was so weak he struggled to pull himself up, but he used the metal table to steady himself, and soon he was standing. When he saw Eleanor, he felt a surge of rage that gave him the strength to climb onto the table. He loomed over Eleanor and tried to muster the strength to do what he had to do.

Eleanor did not seem fully awake, but her face was changing. Her eyes bulged. Black tentacles shot from her mouth, from her fingers, from her toes. The slimy black vines climbed up the walls and slithered over the floor. Tentacles flew from her and wrapped around his face until he couldn't see.

In the warehouse, Larson tried to push Eleanor off him, but she had him pinned, and she leaned down and bit his cheek, drawing blood, then laughing. He shivered from the sound and the pain.

Larson managed to roll over so that he was now on top of Eleanor. His hands closed around her throat.

In the living room, Jake dodged the black blood that spewed from Eleanor's nose and mouth. Eleanor sat bolt upright and grabbed his neck with both hands. Jake felt a sudden surge of strength. He pulled her hands away as if he were doing nothing more strenuous than swatting a fly.

Holding Eleanor's wrists, Jake loomed over her, his eyes burning with fury. He leaned over her until her face and torso were covered by his cloak. She twisted and kicked, but he just pressed in closer, eyes blazing with fury, burning into Eleanor until she was still.

Jake knew that only he could hear Eleanor's roaring fury now. She wasn't animated anymore. She was part of Jake, the same way Andrew had been. But she wasn't like Andrew.

Andrew hadn't been nice, exactly. He'd been as full of rage as Eleanor was. But Andrew had just been hurt. He hadn't been bad at the core.

Eleanor *was* bad at the core. But she had no power here.

Jake concentrated until he was able to access Eleanor's memories . . . if they could be called memories.

Using the ability that Jake had discovered after his confrontation with the trash rabbit, Jake reached into those years and found a moment of seething anger and anguish. He figured if he could stuff Eleanor into a bubble of that moment, he could subdue her.

He was right. With that one intention, Eleanor was defeated, contained. Her foul spirit folded in on itself and was silenced.

When Jake saw her lying on the table, she had the dry, withered appearance of an ancient mummy. She was more than dead. She was empty. A husk.

Exhausted, Jake lay back and let his mind go blank.

Two Weeks Later:

Larson was no longer destined to wander around lost in different places and times. He was in the here and now, which in this case was the ball field at the time of his son's game. The air was crisp, but the sky was so blue it looked like the painted backdrop of a play.

Larson's fights with Eleanor had opened some stitches, so he was bandaged up again. Stiff and sore, Larson gingerly climbed into the bleachers and took a seat at the end of a row. He looked out over the green diamond. There was Ryan. He was in the outfield, and as often was the case with Ryan, he looked bored. He was playing with his baseball glove and kicking at the grass with one shoe, which appeared to be untied.

Larson grinned when Ryan looked up into the stands and spotted his dad. Ryan waved wildly, and Larson waved back. Then Larson pointed at the batter. Still grinning, Ryan nodded and focused on the task at hand.

The batter at the plate took a swing and connected.

Crack!

Under the bright sun, the ball soared toward the outfield. Larson stood, cheering when his son caught the ball.

Jake wasn't sure why he felt so drawn to the abandoned restaurant, but he did. So much so that with what little strength he had left, he'd painstakingly made his way across town to get here.

His battery had recharged, just a little, enough for him to walk. But his walk was actually more of a shuffle; he wasn't going to make it far. Every movement took all the strength Jake possessed.

Now Jake pushed inside the empty building. His feet dragged across the dusty floor as he aimed toward his destination. In a way, she was leading him here, he knew. But not really. She had no will left. He was in control. But he'd learned enough about her as he'd over-come her to know that this was where she had to be laid to rest.

Jake shuffled across a barren dining room and made his way to the ball pit he'd been seeing in his mind's eye since he'd integrated Eleanor's remains into his consciousness. It was a horrible place. He could tell. Not just that it looked horrible—all dusty and faded and smelling of decay—but it *was* horrible. It was like a graveyard for the souls of victims of a wicked wrongness that he didn't fully understand. What had happened here? Where did Eleanor come from? Had she caused all this chaos, or had the chaos somehow caused her?

Jake paused in front of the dingy yellow rope that warned away anyone crazy enough to come in here and try to enter this pit of terror and pain. This was where Jake had to be to do the last bit of good he could do. It felt kind of like the end, but he hoped it was going to be more of a beginning—the start of the one journey he really wanted to take.

He'd finished everything he'd had to do. He'd managed to reunite Dr. Talbert with his real daughter. And he'd found the real homeless girl Eleanor had replaced. The *real* girl with the reddish-brown hair had been locked in a trunk in the abandoned building where Jake had originally found Eleanor. Depsite her terror at being rescued by him, he'd made sure she got to a hospital.

Jake stepped into the ball pit, and as soon as he did, the pit started taking him. He let the ball pit pull him down. And down. And down. It felt kind of like sinking into a pool of water. All he had to do was relax and let himself drift downward.

So that's what he did. He sank lower and lower. As soon as he did, he was no longer aware of the pit. He wasn't aware of anything physical at all.

Millie flinched when a low-hanging fir branch brushed against her cheek. She batted it away and peered into the darkness beyond it. Where was her grandpa's house? She'd just been there, hadn't she? How could she have gotten this lost?

Millie tugged her black sweater tighter around her. She rubbed her arms to get warm. She felt really chilled—even though the night wasn't that cold.

Before she'd left the house, she hadn't wanted to be at the stupid Christmas dinner with all her stupid relatives. But now, for reasons she didn't understand, that was the *only* place she wanted to be.

And, of course, because she wanted it, she couldn't have it. She never got what she wanted. She was always forced to do what everyone else wanted her to do. Her parents. Her grandpa. The teachers at school. It wasn't fair.

Nearby, a crow cawed. Millie jumped and spun around. She heard a rustling in the undergrowth, and she tried to see into the darkness.

When nothing moved, she started walking again.

Millie thought she'd only been out here for a few minutes. So why did it feel like she'd been wandering for a very long time?

Before she could ponder that question, the foliage

rustled again, and this time, a hand reached through it. Millie gasped and stopped dead.

A little boy was stepping out from the middle of a huckleberry bush. Millie stared at him, poised to run if he was a threat.

He didn't look like a threat, though. With a round freckled face, bright green eyes, a big smile, and a thick tangle of brown curls that fell into his eyes, the boy looked really nice actually. Millie found herself smiling at him, in spite of herself.

"You lost?" the boy asked.

Millie shook her head even though she was.

"I'm Jake," the boy said. Then he took Millie's hand.

To her surprise, Millie didn't resist at all. Instead, she let the boy—Jake—lead her through the woods.

He didn't lead her for long, though. In what felt like an instant, Jake was there and then gone. He disappeared, and Millie found herself on her grandpa's front porch.

Through the big picture window, Millie could see her family gathering around the table. Behind them, the Christmas tree was lit up just like it had been when she'd left the house. And for some reason, Millie was happy to see it. She was happy to see her family, too.

Not sure why she felt so good all of a sudden—but not really caring, Millie rushed across the porch. She threw open the door and ran into the room. Her grandpa greeted her with a smile and a hug, which Millie . . . for once . . . was happy to receive.

For the first time she could remember, Millie felt like she was home.

Inside the abandoned restaurant, dust motes danced in the silence. The ball pit hunkered in the corner as usual—totally still.

Or, maybe not totally.

Although the plastic balls weren't moving, suddenly, one of them lit up. It lit up and turned from ruddy red to shining gold. Then it turned clear, like a sparkling crystal ball.

Within the glistening glass orb, a tiny scene flared into view. The scene was that of a family Christmas—laughing people gathered around a table near a Christmas tree. In the center of the group of people, a young girl dressed all in black smiled as if she hadn't smiled in a long time.

Around this bright clear ball and its inviting scene, other balls in the ball pit began morphing from filthy plastic to brilliant transparent glass. Every glass ball lit up with its own little happy scene.

Soon all the plastic balls were shimmering. They all twinkled like dazzling stars in a clear night sky.

Larson sat in Dr. Talbert's living room. It seemed strange to be sitting on the sofa in the very room where he had lain on the floor as the Stitchwraith finally put an end to Eleanor. At that time he would have said he would never return to this house.

But he had to. He was a detective, and he still had questions.

Dr. Talbert sat in the armchair across from him. "How can I help you, Detective?"

"There was just one more thing I wanted to clear up," Larson said. "It's out of my own personal curiosity, really. Remnant—what is it? Is it some kind of . . . magic?"

As a younger man, Larson would never have thought magic was even a vague possibility. But he had seen lots of strange things since then.

Talbert sighed. "Remnant is . . ." He paused.

"In nonscientific terms, it's like the metal is haunted. It's more complicated than that, of course, but it's similar to the way that water conducts electricity. Remnant is the mixing of the tangible with the intangible, of memory with the present. The people and things that are lost—it makes them almost real again." Talbert had a sad, faraway look in his eyes. "You know, when Renelle was a little girl, she was sick. She was in and out of the hospital on an almost-constant basis. I was scared—terrified, really—that she would die. I stayed up nights trying to think of ways to protect her. I made this little pendant for her out of Remnant. That way, I figured I could never lose her entirely."

"Do you still have the pendant?" Larson asked.

"Yes. Would you like to see it?"

Larson nodded.

Talbert left the room and came back holding a chain from which a heart-shaped pendant dangled. He held it at a distance from his body, between his finger and thumb, the same way one might hold a dead mouse by the tail. Still, the necklace looked like an ordinary piece of jewelry any young girl might wear. Larson was sure no one ever gave it a second glance.

"It was a terrible mistake to create this," Talbert said, looking down at the necklace. "It was my obsession in creating this that caused me to lose Renelle in the first place."

"I'm afraid I still don't understand," Larson said. "If it's haunted, then haunted by what?"

Talbert didn't meet Larson's eyes. He held out the pendant. "Here, why don't you take it?"

Larson was confused. "Me?"

"Yes," Talbert said. "Take it. Do what you want with it. I honestly can't even bear to look at it anymore."

Talbert dropped the pendant into Larson's palm. It felt so small, so insignificant.

Talbert walked Larson to the door. "Thank you for stopping by, Detective. And thank you for taking the pendant off my hands. Maybe now I can turn the page and start a new chapter in my life, with my real daughter."

Once Larson was on the sidewalk, he heard a soft, high-pitched sound. He looked around for the source of the noise and discovered it was coming from the pendant in his palm. It was like it was singing a song but too softly for Larson to make out the words. He held up the pendant to inspect it, and the sun shone through it. It was dazzling.